Pretty Poison:

"A Fantastic amateur sleuth." ~ The Best Reviews
"Smartly penned and charming garden mystery." ~
Romantic Times

Fruit of the Poisoned Tree:
"I can't recommend this book highly enough."~ Midwest
Book Reviews
"I love the world of Peggy Lee!" ~ Fresh Fiction

Poisoned Petals:
"Joyce and Jim are a fabulous team who create poignant,
entertaining mysteries." ~ The Best Reviews
"An enjoyable and cozy read." The Muse Book Reviews

Perfect Poison:
"A fabulous whodunit!" ~ Fresh Fiction
"You will enjoy this to no end! Highly recommended!" ~
Mystery Scene Magazine

A Corpse for Yew:

"Awesome story with good and rational twists! Love that it
tells about places I know! And there is some great plant
info at the same time!" ~ Snows Acre
"Joyce and Jim Lavene prove once again they are an
excellent writing team as they provide a quality regional
whodunit." ~ Harriet Klausner
A Thyme to Die:

"Totally enjoy this character and the series. Not only are
these good stories, but I learn something about plants and
both their care and uses." ~ Gillian F. Brunner
"There are plenty of twists and turns to keep you guessing.
" ~ Cheryl Green

Killing Weeds

By

Joyce and Jim Lavene

Book coach and editor—Jeni Chappelle
http://www.jenichappelle.com/

Rhododendron
*The first rhododendron to be classified and named was
the Alpine Rose. It was discovered by the 16th century
Flemish botanist, Charles l'Ecluse and introduced to
Britain in 1656. The Japanese were raising rhododendron
hybrids in the 17th century, known as Satsuki Azaleas
today.*

Chapter One

At four-twelve a.m., Peggy Lee's cell phone buzzed.
She sighed, turned over, and tried to go back to sleep.

"Don't you need to get that?" her husband, Steve,
asked in a husky whisper.

"No. It's Sam's turn to find out if a bird flew into a
window at the garden shop and apologize to the police for
bringing them out for nothing." She patted his side. "It's
early. We don't have to get up yet."

He put his arm around her. "Not *that* early." He kissed
the side of her neck. "We could be awake but not get up."

She turned back to him with a smile. "But you have
that conference today. You'll be exhausted if you don't go
back to sleep."

Steve drew her closer. "So I'll be tired, but it'll be
worth it."

Peggy kissed him, but her cell phone sounded again—
this time ringing.

"That can't be good." She picked up her phone from

the bedside table. Sam Ollson's face came up on the screen. He was her partner at their garden shop, The Potting Shed. "Good morning. I guess something big happened."

"You have to get down here, Peggy. You're never gonna believe this." Sam didn't give anything away.

"Okay. I know you wouldn't do this to me if it wasn't important." She yawned, and put down her cell phone. "I've gotta go to the shop, Steve. I guess I'll see you later. Rain check?"

"You bet." He kissed her slowly. "Definitely rain check. What's up?"

She had already slipped away and was finding clothes to wear. "I don't know. But you know how unflappable Sam is. It must be bad for him to want me down there too."

Peggy hurriedly pulled on jeans and a green Potting Shed T-shirt. She brushed her white tinged red locks and rolled her expressive green eyes at her image before she stuck her feet in sandals, grabbed her handbag, and went downstairs.

Her Great Dane, Shakespeare, followed her every move with an inquisitive look on his intelligent face.

"Sorry." She patted his massive head. "I'll be back in a few minutes. You can come next time. Steve will let you out before he leaves today if I'm not back in time."

He made a soft whining sound and pushed at her hand with his nose. She bent and kissed him goodbye before she walked out the door.

Even though Sam was Peggy's partner, The Potting Shed was *her* baby. She'd opened it with her first husband's life insurance policy and every penny she could scrape together. He'd been killed working as a homicide detective for the Charlotte-Mecklenburg Police Department.

John Lee had a strong affinity for growing things, as

Peggy did. It had been their joint dream to open an urban garden center in downtown Charlotte, North Carolina. After his death, she'd put all their resources into getting the business going. It had been lean at first, but as the years passed, she'd developed a strong customer base.

Sam had come onboard later after working for her for a few years. His participation in the landscaping part of their business was flourishing and had been vital to the shop staying alive.

Peggy pulled her car in the parking area behind The Potting Shed. The shop was located in Brevard Court behind Historical Latta Arcade. It looked as though every light was on inside the shop. Dozens of blue and white police cars were parked on the street.

Her heart pounded as she realized that this was no random incident. Something big had happened that could be disastrous to her livelihood.

Sam met her at the stairs. Two stern police officers that she didn't recognize held out their hands to keep her from joining him.

"It's okay, guys," Sam said. "This is the owner of the shop. Let her through."

They moved aside with curt nods in her direction.

Peggy sighed as she realized how many new police officers didn't know her from John's time on the force. Every time she went to the downtown office where he had once worked, there were always officers she'd never met. It felt odd and still slightly unreal to her even though he had been dead for many years.

"What happened?" she whispered to Sam as he put his hand on her arm to help her up the metal stairs that crawled along the side of the old red brick building.

Sam was a big man, more than six feet tall, with massive shoulders and a broad chest. He'd always been large, but years of hard physical labor had made him more muscled. He wore his long blond hair tied away from his handsome face and bright blue eyes, a gentle soul who loved plants as much as Peggy.

"Someone broke into The Potting Shed."

"What did they take? I closed last night. There was only about a hundred dollars in the register. I suppose they got the laptop."

On the steel landing that met the open door, Sam stopped and stared earnestly into her face. "I don't know if I can prepare you for this or not. I almost lost it when I walked in and saw everything. Just remember, we have insurance. Okay?"

She was even more afraid after his warning. What could be in there that Sam would be so upset about? He never lost it—well, almost never.

They walked in through the back door which led into the storage area where large bags of peat moss and heavy items like shovels, wheelbarrows, and the like were kept. Sam also stored live plants here for landscaping the next day. She knew he had a large job coming up with one of the million-dollar houses on Queens Road.

Peggy gasped when she saw the devastation. Every plant and shrub that Sam had purchased for the job had been hacked to pieces. Dirt and plant matter were scattered everywhere. Dozens of rhododendrons had been destroyed. Not a single thing was spared. There was nothing usable left of the expensive shipment.

She blinked back tears, as much from her amazement that anyone could do such a thing as her monetary loss. Sam was right. They had insurance that would cover this. The job would have to be put off. The customer wouldn't like it, but they'd get through it.

"It looks like someone just went crazy in here," Sam said. "Lucky for me that Mrs. Hood is a very nice and understanding lady. She'll be willing to give me time to order more plants for her yard."

. The heart of pine floors squeaked as they walked across them into the front of the shop from the storage area. Everywhere they looked was complete chaos and destruction.

"I'm so sorry about this," Sergeant Eve Malcolm said when she saw Peggy. "Sam said he didn't think anything was actually missing. There's still money in the cash drawer. It looks like this was just serious vandalism."

Peggy knew Eve well. She'd been a rookie just starting out when John was still alive.

"I don't understand how so much damage was done." Peggy looked at her broken rocking chair. Every shelf had been emptied and smashed to pieces. Each box of fertilizer and plant spikes were destroyed too. Everything was gone. "As soon as the person broke in, the security alarm should've been activated. They wouldn't have had enough time to do all this."

"I've made a note of that." Eve's dark eyes glanced at Sam. "We don't know the answer to that yet. We were actually alerted to the break-in by one of your neighbors in the shops. We never got word from the alarm company."

Sam walked over to the front door. "You can see someone wanted to make a statement with this."

Peggy examined the wood and glass door that looked as though it had been hit with an axe or a sledgehammer. The lights were on at The Kozy Kettle Tea and Coffee Emporium across the courtyard. No doubt she had her friends and neighbors Emil and Sofia Balducci to thank for alerting the police. They were in early every morning to bake their wonderful pastries for the day.

"This doesn't seem like something a few teenagers did for fun," Peggy remarked.

"I know some raunchy teenagers who do things a lot worse than this," Eve confided, her dark hair cut in a pageboy style swinging in front of her face as she moved.

"I'll definitely check with the alarm company though. All of you here in the arcade use the same company, don't you?"

Sam lifted the smashed alarm touchpad that had been severed and dropped to the floor. "This should've activated an immediate response."

Eve acknowledged his concern. "We'll get to the bottom of this, Sam. I promise. For now, make a good inventory of your losses, and contact your insurance company. I'll get back with you after we've processed the scene and I have some answers from the alarm company."

She handed Peggy and Sam business cards. "If you think of anyone who could have done this—maybe a competitor or a disgruntled employee—let me know."

There were two men and a woman wearing crime scene jump suits already searching through the rubble for clues. They nodded to Peggy.

The only thing that had remained intact was Peggy's pond. The little pond was still full of water. All the expensive water plants had been yanked out and strewn around the room. Even the seven pretty koi had been taken out of the water and left to die on the floor.

"I don't think they got the lizard, do you?" Peggy carefully searched around the pond, but there was no sign of the lizard that lived there, alive or dead. She took a ragged breath, and wiped her eyes.

Sam put his arm around her. "There's nothing we can do here right now."

"Eve said we should do inventory. I'll look for paper and a pen."

"Let's get out of here and let them work. We can come back later and do inventory. I don't know about you, but I could use a cup of coffee. I'll make you some tea, and we'll be okay."

She nodded, not trusting herself to speak. "You're right. Let's go home."

Hellebore
Also known as the Christmas rose. The black hellebore is a perennial with dark, smooth leaves and white blossoms that are a favorite in gardens. It is deadly poisonous, thus its Greek origins, elein (to injure) and bora (food).

Chapter Two

They went back to Peggy's house on Queens Road. The lights were on inside. Steve was walking Shakespeare in the early spring chill.

Most of the old houses that surrounded theirs in the historic Myer's Park area were dark and quiet. A few cars had begun their workday traffic patterns, hustling into the downtown area of the city.

When Peggy saw Steve and Shakespeare, she wiped her eyes and held it together long enough to tell him what she'd found at the shop. Sam's voice wavered, too, as he added to her story.

Steve Newsome was Peggy's second husband. She'd been alone for years when she'd met him. She never expected to marry again. How could she find a man that she'd love as she had loved John?

But while John and Steve were very different—and Steve was ten years younger than her—love had found her again in the form of this vibrant man.

He immediately put his arms around her and held her tightly. "I'm so sorry. Is there anything I can do?"

Sam shook his head, rubbing his nose with his hand. "I don't think so. The FBI doesn't look into vandalism, do they?"

Steve was also part of law enforcement, and had even worked with John a few times before his death. He'd recently revealed that fact to Peggy when he'd been named director for the Charlotte bureau office.

"I can't look into it professionally," Steve agreed. "But I can help clean up."

"No." Peggy grabbed a tissue out of her bag. "You're going to the conference for the next two days. If there's something else to clean when you get back, I'll stick a broom in your hand."

"I'm not leaving you like this." The expression in his dark brown eyes was serious. "They can get along without me. I'm staying until you get through it."

Peggy wiped her eyes and blew her nose. "Don't be silly. Sam, Selena, and I can handle it. We'll inventory everything for the police and the insurance company. I'll have to send an email to all our customers and let them know we'll be closed for a few days. But I'll be fine. No one died—except the fish. We'll be okay."

"Peggy's right," Sam said. "It's just a mess, Steve. But we'll take care of it, and I'll take care of her until you get back. I just hope we find out who did this. I don't care if it's a teenager or not. I'm kicking some ass."

Steve shook his hand. "You have my cell phone number. Call me if you need anything. Thanks."

Peggy hugged him and fussed with his tobacco brown hair that was a little longer than he usually wore it. She straightened his blue tie, and kissed him.

She could see he was ready to go, his suitcase at the

door. "He's right. Everything will be fine. It was just such a surprise. And don't worry. I'll take care of Sam while you're gone."

"All right. I guess I'm going then." Steve kissed Peggy and hugged her. "I love you. Don't let me come back and find the two of you skulking around looking for whoever did this. Let the police do their job. Okay?"

She smiled into his warm eyes. "Okay."

"Really, Peggy." He glanced at Sam. "You too."

"We're not going after anyone," she promised. "Unless he has a large garbage container to hold the debris."

Sam and Peggy waved as they watched Steve's SUV leave the driveway.

"Are we gonna look for who did this?" Sam asked.

"Only after coffee and tea," she responded.

"Then I could do with some toast too."

"And some toast." She smiled as she went into the house and put on water for tea.

She fed Shakespeare, playing with his floppy ears as she did. When she'd rescued him, he'd been older than the usual pup when they had their ears cropped. She didn't have the heart to have it done after everything he'd been through. He looked beautiful to her.

Sam and Peggy strategized over bagels with cream cheese and fresh strawberries.

"I don't know how we'll figure out who did this," Peggy said. "Unless the police come up with a suspect from fingerprints or some other evidence, I can't imagine who'd do such a thing."

Sam swirled his strawberry in sugar before popping it into his mouth. "What about that man a few weeks ago who gave Selena such a hard time?"

"I don't think a man who was disappointed because we couldn't get the pink and white hellebore he wanted would trash The Potting Shed. Either this was a kid thing or someone has a serious problem with us."

He snapped his fingers. "What about Mrs. Stanton? I wouldn't do her yard last month, remember? She's rich. Maybe she hired someone."

"Maybe." Peggy finished her bagel and wiped her hands on a napkin. "Do you want me to go with you to explain to Mrs. Hood about what happened?"

"No. I'll be fine. It's not like it's going to cost her any extra money. We'll have to absorb that cost until the insurance kicks in."

"I know. I guess I was just offering emotional support. She'll hear about it on the news, probably."

"Yeah. Speaking of which, I'd better go home and change. I'm supposed to be working at her house at eight this morning. You should call Selena, I guess. Want to meet back at The Potting Shed at ten to do the inventory?"

"Sure. That'll be fine."

She hugged Sam and thanked him for being there. She knew he felt as bad as she did about all the dead plants. He might be big and reminded people of Thor, but he had a soft heart.

Peggy watched him leave, but he'd only been gone a moment when her next door neighbor scooted in through her still-open door.

"Walter? I'm surprised to see you so early."

Walter Bellows grinned and took Sam's spot at her kitchen table. "Any tea left? What a terrible night. I heard the whole thing on the police scanner."

He removed his tweed cap so that little tufts of his gray hair sprang up all over his head. He was a tiny man with a bird-like countenance who'd only been Peggy's neighbor for a few years.

"I have one cup left." She poured it for him. "The shop was a mess."

"So I understood. I saw Steve leave earlier. Is he going

to get the FBI to help you?"

"The FBI doesn't do things like that." She sat with him for a moment. "I have a lot of things I have to do today, Walter. The shop won't be open, but there's the insurance and police matters to resolve."

"Any idea who did it?" He grabbed the last strawberry on the plate. "Need any help sussing him out?"

"I don't have a clue. I wish I did. I think we'll have to spend today recovering from it before I can really worry about who did it."

"But aren't the first few hours critical to finding the suspect?" His puffy gray brows met above his sallow face and pale blue eyes.

Peggy hadn't always been friends with Walter. They'd had many disagreements after he'd moved next door. But she'd found they had more in common than she'd thought. He was a plant lover too, and a botanist like her.

"Unless the police find something to track the people who did this, I'm at a loss. But if I'm going to 'suss out' the person, I'll be sure to let you know."

He rubbed his hands together. "Thank you. You know how I enjoy your little excursions into the forensic field. I even took the same forensic botany class that you did in Raleigh. If something ever happens to you, the police may call upon me."

She laughed. "I'll be sure to let them know."

Her cell phone rang as she was gently trying to shoo Walter from the house so she could leave. The call came from the Charlotte-Mecklenburg police so she assumed it had something to do with the vandalism.

Instead, it was John's old partner—now a homicide lieutenant—Al McDonald.

"Hey, Peggy. I have a case right up your alley. Can you come and take a look at a murder over on Providence Road?"

Hakone Forest Grass

A handsome Japanese perennial that is long-lived and grown around the world, prized for its long, slender leaves and not growing wildly outside its planted area.

Chapter Three

Peggy didn't bother changing clothes. Usually she dressed in something more office casual for her forensic botany work for the city. With the day she'd had so far, jeans and a T-shirt seemed to be appropriate.

She was glad Walter went home without much argument. He was excited by the prospect of another case for her with the medical examiner's office. Peggy was their contract forensic botanist. It was only a part-time job when the ME believed she needed advice on anything to do with plants that could influence a police investigation.

She'd taken the forensics course years ago out of curiosity rather than expecting to make much money from the work. Her specialty had evolved into poisonous botanicals after she'd finished college. She looked at the forensic botanist job as an extension of that, and it was fascinating.

Peggy frequently led workshops and programs for local law enforcement on how to know if they were dealing with something in her field of expertise as well as how to collect and store potentially poisonous plants. It was fulfilling to her, even though her schedule could get hectic at times.

Al had called her to a huge building filled with luxury condos. The whole place looked like a castle. The grounds were beautifully landscaped with all the neatly trimmed flowering trees and shrubs that one would expect. There were flowering pear and cherry trees. Remnants of their blossoms drifted to the sidewalk at her feet. There was bright yellow Hakone forest grass that artfully draped close to the walkway without touching it and square holly bushes that barely reached a foot tall.

Police officers were at the front door to the building. She'd seen their cars on the street before she'd parked. Two young officers—maybe their first time out—were stationed there to check IDs before allowing anyone inside.

Peggy didn't know them and had to show her ID from the medical examiner's office. They waved her through, and another officer handed her covers for her shoes and gloves. She took a paper mask from him with a smile, though she didn't think it would be necessary to use it and then followed the trail of officers to the eighth floor.

Al was waiting for her, having been notified by the front door officers that she'd arrived. The police seemed to be on their best behavior in this case, perhaps because of the high-dollar housing they were investigating.

"Peggy." He smiled and hugged her. He'd been on a diet since his last doctor's visit and had lost ten pounds. It didn't show yet on his heavyset body or his thick, muscular neck, but he said it made him feel better.

"Everyone is so polite and quiet," she mentioned. "They're doing everything but tiptoeing and whispering. This is a beautiful place. I guess they're impressed."

"It's nice enough." He glanced at the heavy wood paneling that covered the walls. "I'd rather be out at my old fishing cabin than live here. How could anyone think of a place like this as home?"

She laughed. "I'm sure Mary would love it. The carpet is nice."

"Whatever." He started walking away from the elevator. "We've got a weird one."

"Which is why I'm here."

"That's right. I hate the weird ones as much as I like seeing you."

"I know you do. John always did too."

He smiled at her. "I think he'd get a kick out of you doing this."

"I'd like to think so." It was years after John had been killed during a domestic dispute before she'd started working with the police. She really wasn't sure how he would have felt about her job. Would he have been comfortable working with her?

Al looked at his notebook. "We have one dead woman. Ms. Nita Honohan. Mid-thirties, about five-five. Dyed blond hair. Obviously well-to-do. She's lived here since the building opened. She was originally from New York. Owned some kind of business. We're looking into that."

"How did she die?"

"That's why you're here." He grinned at her. "You don't make the big bucks with no effort. Uh-uh. Mai's got this one. She's waiting inside."

The large condo Peggy stepped into was as beautiful and carefully appointed as the outside hall and the entry downstairs. Everything appeared new and thoughtfully arranged. It seemed the building interior designer had very good, very expensive taste.

There were dozens of police officers and crime scene techs scattered throughout the three-bedroom condo. Two of them were closely examining the large balcony. There was one brilliantly red begonia out there. It was the perfect spot for it to make the most of the sun.

"Over here!" Mai Sato-Lee, the assistant medical examiner, waved to her. She was standing next to the covered body on the carpet.

"Good morning. You're out early."

"Yeah. Paul had to take Rosie to daycare. I usually do it so I get that time with her."

Mai was married to Peggy's son, Paul. Peggy had become a grandmother last year and found that it was the most glorious occupation of all.

"I can't wait until playtime Thursday afternoon," Peggy said. "She's such a sweetie. And a lovely combination of you and Paul."

Mai was Vietnamese. Her huge, almond-shaped brown eyes and pretty face complimented Paul's green eyes and red hair. Rosie was a wonderful combination of the pair.

"Yes." Mai cleared her throat as she glanced self-consciously around the crowded room. "I'm glad you're here Dr. Lee. We have an unusual death. I think there may be something you can contribute. I've never seen anything like it."

Peggy steeled herself as Mai carefully crouched beside the victim and pulled back the sheet. It had never become second nature to see people in their final throes of life. No one should have to be on exhibit this way. No one should ever be killed by another human being.

This one was particularly gruesome. The woman had obviously been in terrible pain when she'd died. Her face and body were contorted, parts of her dress and coat ripped away from her body. But there was very little blood.

Peggy was horrified. And intrigued. She knelt on the carpet beside her daughter-in-law. "How did she die?"

The victim was dressed as though she was ready to go

out. Her makeup was perfect. She still wore stylish black heels.

Ms. Honohan was also wearing a full-length mink coat. It looked new, but it was hard to say since she seemed to have taken very good care of her things.

Everywhere the coat had touched her left the skin red with some kind of chemical burn. The worst of it was on her torso where her dress and skin had almost melted into the lining of the fur.

"She was trying to get the coat off," Peggy said. "Something in it burned her."

"We were thinking formaldehyde when we first got here," Mai said. "People have been known to be poisoned by clothes that still have formaldehyde in them if they wear them without adequate cleaning."

Peggy shook her head. "No. Look at her. She didn't get this coat from a secondhand store. And formaldehyde wouldn't have this effect. I can't smell anything, can you?"

Mai agreed there was no scent. "But the only thing I could think of was an organic poison. What else could do something like this? I'll have it tested, but I don't think it's acid. If it was, why wouldn't it burn through the coat too?"

"I'll need some samples." Peggy studied the beautiful young victim as Mai sent one of the lab techs to fetch a sample container. She'd had everything going for her. How terrible that this had happened to her.

Was it a murder, as Mai and Al had surmised, or was it a terrible mistake?

Eucalyptus
A fast-growing tree, native to Australia. The trees can grow quite tall and have an interesting bark and fragrance. The leaves have been used for generations as a medicinal.

Chapter Four

Peggy had seen too many careless mistakes with botanicals in recent years. People didn't understand that plants and their extracts could be deadly. They used plant chemicals they knew nothing about in ways they were never meant to be used. Hadn't she recently read a case of a woman accidentally using eucalyptus to burn out her sinuses?

Mai handed Peggy a sealed sample container and a thin wood stick that she was supposed to use to scrape off some of the goo that was between the victim and her coat.

It was part of her job to gather this evidence, but Peggy didn't like it. Her work was centered on plants—how to grow them and how to improve them. Forensic work was fascinating, but could also be disgusting.

She carefully used the tiny wood spatula to push a little of what was left of the woman's skin and clothes into the container. Mai quickly sealed it and wrote her name, the date, and time on it.

"Maybe you should get one more while you're there." Mai handed her another container and another spatula. "It's good to have two samples, right?"

Peggy agreed and got the sample before she got back on her feet.

"I can see why you thought it was acid," she said to Mai. "Actually, the material is completely smeared on the inside of the coat. It's where it came into contact with the skin that burned her."

"Cause of death was probably shock from chemical or biological burns," Mai said. "I hope never to see anything like this again."

Peggy was still scanning the woman on the floor. On the right sleeve of the mink was a tag.

"I think the store tag is still on the coat." She glanced around the room. "And there's the box it came in."

She and Mai went over to it. The large box was open, both halves on the expensive silk sofa.

"Stewart's." Mai wrote it down and took a picture. "We'll have to examine the box for any residue of what's in the coat. Looks like she got it today, tried it on, and it killed her."

"I guess she didn't try it on at the store," Peggy said. "Maybe she ordered it online and it was delivered here."

Al came to stand with them by the box. "Ladies. Anything interesting?"

Mai confidently told him their theory. "I guess you should check with the store, huh? And the lobby downstairs. Maybe there's a video of someone selling it to her or bringing it up here."

He wrote what she said. "Thanks. Careful now. We'll be like one of those forensic shows on TV, and I'll be out of a job."

"I'm not carrying a gun," Mai said. "Sorry. I didn't

mean to step on your part of the investigation, Al."

Peggy knew Mai was excited and nervous about being there. She was only an assistant medical examiner. "Where's Dr. Beck?"

"She's at a conference," Mai explained the whereabouts of the ME. "It's been a while since I had to take over for her. It makes me worry that I'm not doing something right."

"Steve's at a conference too," Peggy said. "Maybe they're at the same conference."

Mai's brown eyes widened. "That's not what I meant. I'm sure Dr. Beck isn't at a conference with Steve. I mean, they wouldn't be there together."

Al laughed and patted her arm. "Don't worry about it. You're doing a good job. I'm sure Steve and Dr. Beck would get a good laugh out of the idea that they met for something besides business at a conference. I'm going to send someone downstairs to see if there's video of people going in and out."

Mai's pretty face was red. It had become a little rounder since she'd been pregnant with her daughter, Rosie. "I'm sorry I didn't understand what you meant, Peggy."

"Don't be silly. I was just teasing you. Is there anything else you'd like me to do while I'm here?"

"No. That's fine. I guess I'll see you later at the lab. I hope you can figure out what killed her."

"Before Dr. Beck comes back, right?" Peggy smiled.

"That would be nice," Mai admitted. "But not necessary."

"Okay. I'll see you later. Say hi to Paul for me if you see him."

Mai looked confused. "You just saw him last night. Is something up with you two?"

Peggy considered her words carefully. She hadn't seen her son last night. Was Paul taking extra shifts to make ends meet? Mai wouldn't like that since she felt that he worked too much anyway.

But if he was going to make her his alibi, he needed to let her know.

"No. Nothing's up. I just worry about him. That's all."

"Oh. Of course. Bye, Peggy."

Peggy left the condo and went back downstairs. A group of concerned tenants were questioning Al about what had happened. Two officers flanked him, but it seemed unlikely the young, well-dressed crowd would get rowdy. She walked around the people in the lobby area and went back out to her car.

She shivered as she got inside, thinking about that poor woman upstairs. She wasn't trained to make deductions about what she saw—only come up with facts about botanical agents that may have been used during a crime.

But if deductions had been her job, she would've considered a toxic mink to be something that involved a crime of passion. Who else would give a woman an expensive coat? She hoped Al checked with the woman's boyfriend or lover. She obviously lived alone but that didn't mean she didn't have someone special in her life.

Peggy checked her phone. There were several messages from her assistant at the garden shop, Selena Rogers. There were also a few messages from Sam.

She didn't want to block anyone in at the condominium and decided she'd wait to answer those messages until she got to The Potting Shed. No doubt she knew what Sam and Selena had to say.

She'd already seen the message from Eve Malcolm that the investigation was complete. That meant cleanup could commence.

The glory of a Southern spring surrounded her as she drove the short distance between Providence Road and

Brevard Court. Colors, smells, and warm days had seemed to erupt all at once, engulfing the city of Charlotte in its embrace.

Peggy marveled at a double flowering, weeping cherry tree on one corner. It was all she could do to stay in the car. Daffodils and tulips lined walkways and porches. Forsythias spilled their bright yellow blossoms in nearly every yard.

It was hard to see these marvels without feeling a lift in her heart. Despite Nita Honohan's death—or maybe because of it—it was wonderful to be alive on such a day.

Traffic was light. The sky was brilliant blue. Peggy sighed and took her time getting to The Potting Shed. It was unheard of for her not to be excited about spending time at her shop, but knowing the destruction that waited for her put a damper on her usual exuberance.

She took the time to appreciate the beauty around her as she organized her thoughts for cleaning and restocking. Should she keep the shop open even though it would mean being embarrassed when a customer asked for something she didn't have? Or should she leave the closed sign up and plan a grand reopening? She could see the merits in both plans.

Brevard Court was busy when she arrived. Even in the back loading area where she parked, there were dozens of cars. Wouldn't it figure that just as people were venturing out of their winter hibernation to enjoy the nice weather, her shop would be closed?

Grabbing her handbag and refusing to allow Sam or Selena to see her sadness about the damage, she put on a bright smile and marched up the metal stairs into the shop.

To her surprise, the back storage area was almost completely clean. The trash was gone, and the concrete floor had been swept. She didn't understand until she saw one of her best customers, Claire Drummond, with a scarf on her head and a broom in her hand.

"Oh, Peggy." Claire hugged her. "I came as soon as I heard. I think I scared Selena because I brought my own cleaning things. But it's just as well because some people didn't think of it, and they needed to use your brooms and such. I'm so sorry someone did this. But we'll have it straightened up in no time."

Peggy was speechless. She stared at Claire, but couldn't think of a single thing to say. She walked into the front of the store where a dozen more customers were picking up shelves and taking out trash.

Walter was there in shorts that were too tight and short. Starr Richards was helping Selena take inventory of what had been destroyed. Emil and Sofia, from across the cobblestones, were handing out free coffee and donuts.

Even one of the FBI agents who worked with Steve, Millie Sanford, was there. She appeared to be giving the dead Koi a proper burial in a shoe box.

"I didn't know if you wanted to bury them or flush them. I thought you could decide when you're ready." Millie hugged her, her straight red hair swinging across her shoulder. "I'm glad I didn't go to the conference. When Steve told me what happened, I came right over. Do they have any idea who did this yet?"

Feeling completely overwhelmed by all the effort on her behalf, Peggy was close to tears. She spoke with each of her friends and thanked them for being there. She answered the question on everyone's minds—so far they had no idea who'd damaged the shop.

Sam came in as everyone was talking and drinking tea or coffee. His handsome face was grim as he asked Peggy to join him outside in the courtyard.

There were benches and tables available for shoppers to take a break and enjoy the historic shopping area. Each of the pots of flowers had a small sign advertising The

Potting Shed since she and Sam took care of them.

Right now there were purple hyacinths and yellow pansies in every pot.

"Can you believe it?" she gushed. "All those people came out to help us. It's amazing, isn't it?"

"Maybe you should sit down, Peggy," Sam said. "Something else has come up."

Trumpet vine
An attractive wild plant in many locations, the trumpet vine flower is loved by hummingbirds and butterflies, but hated by some gardeners who find it invasive, but the plant can be grown with care and kept in its place. The tubular flowers vary in color from yellow to red during the summer. In fall, the plant produces long seedpods.

Chapter Five

After they'd found The Potting Shed completely trashed, and she'd gone to a terrible crime scene, Peggy felt comfortable standing for whatever his bad news was. Maybe Mrs. Hood wasn't willing to wait to have her landscaping done. Maybe she'd hired someone else to do the work. Either way, compared to everything else, she was sure she could handle it.

"What is it?" she asked.

"If you won't sit, maybe I will." Sam collapsed on the cute wood bench next to them, and put his head in his hands.

She sat, too, when she saw how upset he was. "Was Mrs. Hood nasty to you about not getting the job done right away?"

Sam stared hard into her eyes. "Mrs. Hood, who contracted me to work on her landscaping, wasn't Mrs. Hood."

"I don't understand." Peggy could hear laughter and

music from inside. It was awkward being out here knowing her friends were inside cleaning. She wished he'd get it over with.

"I got a call from Mrs. Hood. She wanted me to start doing her landscaping."

"Yes. I know. That was last week."

"That's right. I made an appointment and went to see her. We walked around her yard for an hour as she described what she wanted to change and the plants she wanted to add."

Please get to the point. "Yes. That's what you always do."

"I went to tell her what had happened, and to reschedule. Only the Mrs. Hood that I spoke to a month ago wasn't there."

She understood what he was saying, but couldn't grasp the explanation. "Who was there?"

"Mrs. Hood. The *real* Mrs. Hood, I assume. She didn't look anything like the other woman, and she knew nothing about me doing her landscaping." He pushed a stray lock of hair out of his face in frustration. "I must have sounded like a crazy person. She called her husband and took out her revolver before she showed me her driver's license to prove who she was."

Now he had her complete attention.

"That doesn't make any sense." Peggy tried to get at the heart of it. "Who else would've been there besides the owner?"

"I don't know. But because I knew we were on a timetable, I reordered everything for her before I went back to her house. I thought it would be good to present her with a done deal, you know? Now we've got about ten thousand dollars in plants coming tomorrow, and no one to sell them to. I called, but I couldn't stop it. I'm sorry, Peggy."

She mentally calculated what the loss would be if they couldn't find someone else to take the plants before they were too far gone to survive. It was going to hurt, especially on top of the loss from the vandalism.

Her mind kept coming back to someone impersonating Mrs. Hood to hire Sam for the job. *Why would anyone do such a thing?* "It wasn't the woman who lives next door to the Hoods, was it? Was it some kind of mistaken identity? I guess you only met with Mrs. Hood outside."

He nodded. "We didn't go inside. But you know that's not unusual. I don't know how it happened. It was the right house. I remembered everything she'd said she wanted and where she wanted to put it. I don't know if I'm losing my mind or if we were set up."

"Who would purposely do something like this?"

"I don't know. I already told Sergeant Malcolm about it. I think she was opting for me going crazy. She said she'd get back with me, but what's there to say?"

Peggy got to her feet. "I'm not sure. Let's tell Millie about it. I know she can't actually involve the FBI, but maybe she can shed some light on the matter."

Sam's sister, Hunter, came up the cobblestones as they were about to go inside. She was with off-duty Charlotte Police Officer Luke Blandiss. They'd been dating since he'd given her an expensive speeding ticket last year.

They were a striking couple—tall, beautiful, and fit. He was dark, and Hunter was fair. Heads turned when they walked past shoppers at the other tables in the arcade.

"Hey, you two!" Hunter hugged both of them, a distinctly female version of her brother. "Luke and I came to help. Did the police get anyone for this yet?"

"Maybe the two of you could listen to Sam's story," Peggy suggested. "Hang on a minute while I get someone else in on this. Believe me. It's a lot stranger than someone vandalizing The Potting Shed."

Peggy got Millie as Hunter, Luke, and Sam took a seat

at one of the pretty tables with a colorful umbrella above it on the cobblestone walkway. There was a struggling trumpet vine with delicate orange flowers growing along the edge of the wall beside it.

Sam waited to tell his story until Millie and Peggy were seated too. When he'd finished his tale, each of his listeners had a perplexed frown on their faces.

"That's the craziest thing I've ever heard. Leave it to you to aim for a new high in weirdness," Hunter teased her brother.

Millie and Luke exchanged knowing glances across the table.

Peggy knew that look. "What is it?"

"It's not all that crazy." Millie's brown eyes were intent on her subject. "People scam things like this all the time, although usually there's money or goods that changes hands. What was there for this woman to gain?"

Luke agreed. "Did you give her something to hire you, Sam?"

"No. Nothing besides my time. She didn't give me anything either."

"What about a signed contract for the work?" Hunter, the attorney, asked.

"We don't work that way," Sam said. "We're handshake people. It's always worked for us."

"This might not be anything more than a stupid prank," Luke advised. "Maybe you should consider a contract next time."

Sam nodded.

"But what would be the point of someone doing this?" Peggy asked. "Whoever did it had to know Sam would be back to do the work. Were they standing behind the trees laughing? No one got any money out of it."

"I think it's odd, timed with this extreme vandalism,"

Millie said. "Especially since some knowledge of the alarm system was necessary. Someone was prepared to do this and did a really thorough job of it. Any word from the police about how the alarm was disabled?"

"Not yet," Peggy said. "I know it was cut inside."

"But that should have triggered the alarm," Luke added. "That's the way it works. What's the name of the alarm service that takes care of your shop, Peggy?" "They take care of all the shops in here," she responded.

"I hope you don't mind." Millie frowned. "I took pictures when I first got here."

Peggy nodded. "Steve wanted to see."

"Yes. But I think the events are strange too. It could be coincidence, but maybe not. Who's handling the case?"

"Sergeant Eve Malcolm." Peggy handed her Eve's card. "Whatever you can do, Millie, I appreciate it. I know no one died or anything, but it's quite a financial blow to us."

"Don't forget that scams and other financial crimes can be investigated by the police too," Luke said with a smile. "I'll speak with the sergeant when I go in later."

"Thanks, Luke." Peggy included him too.

"Don't get in trouble," Hunter said

"You don't have to worry about me, baby." Luke kissed her quickly. "Let's go inside and see what we can do, huh?"

The three went into The Potting Shed first.

Peggy held Sam back for a moment. "Don't worry about this. You did what you were supposed to do. Even if you had a contract signed by someone who wasn't Mrs. Hood, what good would it do? It's not like the police would spend time having people match their signatures to it. Let it go, Sam. Let's find out what's really behind this."

"I will. But I have ten thousand dollars' worth of plants I have to find new homes for. I think that will take my mind off of it. Thanks, Peggy."

She hugged him. "It's going to be okay."

But a dread, as her father from Charleston used to say, had settled on her. What in the world was going on?

Crape Myrtle
Though the beautiful crape myrtle is thought to typify Southern states, it is actually native to Asia. Many consider it a native to these shores because it has been here so long. George Washington received seeds to grow on his plantation in 1799.

Chapter Six

Clean up was over quickly with so many hands grabbing brooms and willing to do whatever was necessary. Peggy thanked them all for coming to their rescue.

When everyone else was gone, she smiled at Selena and Sam. "Well, that was the easy part. Now all we have to do is write down everything that was destroyed or stolen."

"That's easy too," Selena declared with a toss of her newly-cut black hair. Her golden brown eyes focused on her laptop. "I have everything right here. We can make a print-out for the insurance company and police from this."

Sam laughed. "Yeah. Right. That's looking at new inventory. What about old inventory?"

"What old inventory?"

"The stuff that hangs around forever. Plastic birds. Trellises. The stuff that doesn't go bad but sells slowly. That stuff. We never throw any of that away, but none of it is any good now."

"I'm sure I've got that too," Selena said confidently.

"We got everything listed that I saw on the floor. I think we're good to go."

"Let me take a look at that." Sam turned the laptop toward him.

The front door opened, and an older gentleman in a neat suit and tie came in.

"I'm sorry. We're closed," Peggy said as Selena and Sam wrangled over the laptop. "We had a break-in last night and lost most of our merchandise. I'll be glad to take your name and information if you'd like me to contact you when we open again. Or I can still take orders."

The man with the neatly trimmed beard stepped forward and shook her hand. "Dr. Lee, I'm guessing. I'm Robert Dean from Gromer's Insurance. I'm sorry about your trouble. I'm here to help if I can."

Peggy liked his open smile. He had a good handshake—not so hard that she felt like he was going to squeeze her hand off but not like she was holding a wet noodle either. He seemed a pleasant person, surprisingly so since he was an insurance adjuster.

"Thank you for coming so quickly, Mr. Dean. We just got the cleanup done. I hope that wasn't a problem for you. We have plenty of pictures of the damage if you need to see it, and the police have even more."

"That's fine." He handed her a business card. "You can send those to my email along with your loss inventory list."

"Thanks." She handed the card to Selena and introduced her assistant and Sam to him. "What else will we need to do to be reimbursed for our loss so we can get the shop up and running again?"

"I'm assuming the police have cleared you in their investigation. I'm afraid I just got into town and haven't had a chance to speak with them on this matter."

"They've finished the investigation here at the shop,"

she told him. "The only question seems to be what happened to the alarm system."

He raised his mostly gray brows that matched the slight gray fringe of his hair. "That's right. You have an alarm. Did the police respond in a timely manner?"

"They responded after someone from The Kozy Kettle across the way phoned it in," Sam answered. "There was nothing from the alarm company."

"It's odd that I haven't heard anything from them today either," Peggy said. "I should probably give them a call. We don't want to stock up again until the alarm is repaired."

"It didn't do much good last time," Selena reminded her.

"I'll have a conversation with them for you, Dr. Lee." Robert Dean checked in his notebook for their information. "It's the least I can do to get this process running smoothly."

"Please, call me Peggy." She smiled at him. "Whatever you can find out would be helpful. I appreciate your being here."

"We'll figure this out, Peggy. And please, call me Bobby. All my customers do."

With another handshake, and a cursory look around the front of the shop, Bobby left.

Selena laughed. "I think Bobby likes you, Peggy. And that was some fine flirting you were doing too."

"Don't be stupid," Sam said. "She wasn't flirting with Bobby. She has Steve."

"Hey. A woman can flirt a little with a nice older gentleman. You never know when that's gonna help your insurance claim. I'm surprised you weren't flirting with him too." Selena always found a way to give Sam a hard time.

"Aren't you supposed to send something to someone?" Sam asked. "I'm going to visit our customers and see if we can unload some of tomorrow's shipment before it gets here."

"Thank you, Sam," Peggy said. "And thank you, Selena. I don't know how I would've gotten through this without the two of you."

"You'd have *Bobby*," Selena suggested with a big grin.

Sam grunted and slammed the back door as he left the shop.

Peggy helped finish the inventory report. Selena sent off the emails, and they left too.

"You don't have to worry about getting a new laptop right away," Selena offered. "We can use mine right now. With spring break, I'm not using it much. Good thing I backed up The Potting Shed's files to my laptop too."

"Thank you," Peggy said. "Do you need a ride somewhere?"

A loud red Mustang pulled into the back lot and a handsome young man leaned out the window. "Hey, beautiful! You almost ready?"

Selena giggled and waved to Peggy. "This is him—Mr. Right. I'll see you later."

"I guess Mr. Right doesn't have a name." She watched them leave, the Mustang spitting out gravel as it tore out of the parking lot.

She got in her car, thinking that if he was really Mr. Right, she'd learn his name later. There had already been many Mr. Rights in the years she'd worked for Peggy.

Selena had accidentally taken one of Peggy's botany classes when she was still teaching at Queens University. Despite not being interested in botany as a profession, Selena had stayed with the class and eventually started working at The Potting Shed for extra money.

Peggy was always glad she had. Selena could be a little flighty at times, but she had a good heart and was wonderful about being there when Peggy needed her.

After getting into the car, Peggy saw there was a text from Mai. The samples she'd taken at the Honohan crime scene were ready to be analyzed.

Peggy tried to call Paul on her way over to the medical examiner's office. Maybe he didn't deserve a heads-up since he hadn't told her or Mai what he'd been doing the night before.

But he was her son. She planned to yell at him for not telling his wife the truth and pry out of him what was really going on.

Relationships that didn't include trust didn't last. She'd hate to see Mai and Paul break up over his need for secrecy, even if he was just working extra hours with the police for the benefit of his family.

But she was even more worried that he might still be trying to find his father's killer. Paul was slightly obsessed with it. He'd decided to become a police officer for that reason, but lately he'd grown more impatient for information.

There was no answer. Peggy left him a text while she sat at a stoplight. The light changed, and she immediately got a loud honk from the driver behind her for her trouble.

The medical examiner's office was a low, flat building with a large parking lot. Peggy parked her car and greeted the landscaper who was mulching soil around a large bed of daffodils, purple hyacinths, and pink tulips. She'd always admired his work on the site—never cutting back the crape myrtles too far or cutting down flowers before they had a chance to set seed.

He pulled at his gray cap. "Thank you, ma'am. People don't much notice the work that goes into keeping things pretty around here. You must be a gardener."

She put out her hand. "Peggy Lee. I own a garden shop in Brevard Court."

"Nice to meet you." He glanced back at the building.

"What are you doing here? Nothing but death in that place."

"I'm a forensic botanist on the side. I guess I love the work because it involves two of my favorite things— puzzles and plants."

"Thanks." He laughed. "I was about to ask what a forensic botanist does."

"I didn't know what it was at first either. But it's a good feeling when we solve a case and give a family the answers they deserve."

"I suppose so." He shook her hand again. "I'm Billy Lowe. If you ever need any help, give me a call."

She promised she would, thinking that Sam might need some extra help if he managed to resell all those plants and shrubs that had been destroyed.

Peggy was yawning as she went inside. Four a.m. was just too early to be up, and stay up all day. She hoped Steve wasn't feeling the same way and smiled as she texted him a yawning emoticon.

"There you are Dr. Lee." Mai uncomfortably glanced around the empty hall. "I'm so glad to see you."

"Everyone around here knows we're related." Peggy put her bag down on her desk. "Even Dr. Beck calls me Peggy. It's okay for you to do it too."

"I have to be more careful than Dr. Beck because I'm not the medical examiner, and she's not your daughter-in-law. I was wondering where you've been."

As Peggy put on her white lab coat, she explained about everything that had been going on at The Potting Shed.

"Is that where Paul was too? I've been trying to reach him all day." Mai walked into the lab with Peggy.

"No. He wasn't with me. I've tried calling him too. With everything the police have to do, I'm sure he's just very busy."

But Peggy's stomach was starting to churn. Where was Paul?

It was probably only because of this other business—it wasn't like she kept track of him every day. He was a grown man. But still . . .

Another worker in the medical examiner's office knocked at the door and then came in. "Dr. Sato, we've gone through all the evidence that was found at the Honohan crime scene and separated it. Do you want to take a look at it now?"

"Sure, Dave. Thank you." Mai smiled at him, but as soon as he was gone she urged Peggy to identify the residue they'd found on Ms. Honohan as quickly as possible.

"Try to remember that this isn't a race." Peggy took the top off one of the plastic containers that contained the gel-like substance from the coat. "It's more important that we're sure than that we're fast. Right?"

"You're right. But it will be a feather in my cap if we're both. Call me when you have something."

Peggy sighed and shook her head as she placed some of the goo on a slide before putting it into the microscope.

Mai had always been ambitious. It wasn't surprising since her parents were the same. They'd expected big things from her, and she was terrified of letting them down. She was the same way with Rosie. She watched everything the baby did with a nervous eye on when she did it and how good she was at it.

Peggy put aside her daughter-in-law's driven nature, and took a close look at the goo they suspected to be botanical. The microscope showed her that not only was the goo plant matter, but she'd seen this phytochemical makeup before.

She hurriedly got on the lab computer to verify her findings, but before she could make a positive ID, Mai came rushing back into the lab.

"When were you going to tell me?" she raged as she stalked back and forth across the green tile floor. "When was *he* going to tell me?"

"I'm not sure what you mean." Peggy felt that strange feeling of dread come over her again.

Mai put a plastic bag with a single business card in it on the counter where Peggy was working. "Paul is a licensed private investigator? What was he doing at Nita Honohan's condo?"

Giant Hogweed

Giant hogweed is a fourteen-foot tall member of the carrot family that makes its home along riverbeds and creeks. Because of the dangerous sap that comes from the plant, gardeners who positively identify it are asked to call for help rather than try to cut the plant by themselves. The sap has been known to burn and blind those who come into contact with it.

Chapter Seven

Peggy picked up the evidence bag and read the private investigator's card in it.

"This has to be some mistake, or a prank," she concluded. "Paul is a full-time CMPD officer. He doesn't have time to be a private investigator on the side."

"Maybe he does," Mai fumed. "Maybe that's why he's never home. And that's why he lied to me about where he was last night."

"Mai—"

"You're a terrible liar, Peggy." She put her hand to her head and gazed absently across the room. "It's bad enough that neither one of us even knew about this, but now he's tied in with this homicide. I'll have to give this to the police. They'll want to question him."

Peggy took off her gloves and went to calm her. "I'm sure there's a rational explanation for this. I know my son. Paul is the worst at keeping secrets. We would've known about this from the moment he first thought about it."

"Will you keep trying to get in touch with him? I don't feel right calling him about the situation when we're investigating the case. I can't believe he'd put me in this position."

"I'm sure this will make more sense once we talk to him." Peggy hopefully consoled Mai—and herself.

"Do we know anything useful about the goo yet?" Mai changed the subject.

"I was about to look it up. I recognize this material. I was at a poison plant symposium last month that dealt with this species aggressively moving across the U.S. I think this might be a hogweed compound."

Mai wrinkled her nose. "Hogweed? What's that?"

"It's a very dangerous plant that's in the carrot family. The plant gets to be eight to ten feet tall."

"That's a big carrot."

"It's very poisonous. It's been in the U.S. for years, but now it's moving further into the country. We expect it to be everywhere in the next few years." Peggy pulled up a file on hogweed. "People are badly burned by the sap from it. They've even gone blind. It creates a burn effect not that much different than some forms of acid. There are terrible blisters that don't go away, sometimes for years."

Mai looked at the pictures on the computer. "And you think this is what caused the burns on Ms. Honohan's body?"

"I think it was the main ingredient in a particularly deadly cocktail of plants that burned her skin so badly that it melted her clothes into it, caused her to go into shock, and die."

"Can you isolate the rest of the compound?"

"I'll see what I can do," Peggy promised.

"But first, get in touch with Paul," Mai said. "He could be involved in this somehow. He could be hurt or dead."

"I'll find him. Don't worry."

Mai hugged Peggy, something unusual for her. She righted her lab coat, nodded, and left the room.

Despite her common sense words to Mai, Peggy was becoming even more nervous.

Finding Paul's PI business card at the crime scene wasn't a good sign. He needed to clear this up before the evidence went from the medical examiner's office to the police department. Mai was right in her estimation of what would happen—Paul would be linked to the murder.

She didn't waste time trying to contact her son again. She called Al and asked him to check on Paul.

If her son was all right, she wanted to hear from him. Peggy didn't explain to her old friend why it was so important that she talk to Paul. Al didn't ask, always happy to help if he could.

Peggy decided there was no point in leaving the ME's office until she heard from Paul. She spent what little time was left of the morning trying to isolate the other plants in the mixture that had coated the inside of the mink Ms. Honohan was wearing.

For a while she was so deeply involved in trying to decide what plant enzymes were in the goo that she forgot about Paul calling her. It startled her when her cell phone rang, and she bumped into the microscope.

It was Steve. He was taking a break at lunch and wanted to thank her for the text she'd sent him. "It was a great reminder of how boring the conference is and how much I want to take a nap."

She smiled at the sound of his voice. "I'm sorry. If I was feeling it, I knew you would be too."

"And I didn't get the fringe benefits from being up too early either since you had to run to the shop," he joked.

Peggy smiled. "Fringe benefits? Is that what they're calling it now?"

Steve's voice was more serious when he changed the

subject. "I took a look at the pictures Millie sent me. That was some job the vandals did at your place. Millie says she's checking into this thing with Sam. Have you heard anything else about it?"

"Not about that." Peggy quickly explained about finding Paul's business card at the murder scene.

"It might not even be *your* Paul Lee," he suggested. "Is it his information?"

Hopefully, Peggy looked at the card again. "There's no address. I don't recognize the phone number. Maybe you're right. I hope you're right for everyone's sake."

"Have you tried calling the number yet?"

"No. Mai and I have been calling Paul all morning, but on his cell phone. I guess we just assumed it was him."

"I have to go. Call the number on the card. Don't assume until you know for sure. I love you. I hope you figure out what's going on."

"I love you too. Thanks for brightening my day."

"You'll figure this out, sweetheart. You always do."

It was lunchtime when she got off the phone. Peggy decided to get out in the sunshine, hoping to de-stress a little. She left her white coat behind and grabbed her handbag. She tried to get Mai to come with her, but she was too anxious about her job and Paul to leave her desk.

Outside, the weather had continued warming. The sunshine was a blessing pouring down on her as she thought about what to eat.

Most days, she met Steve at home for lunch. With him gone, she decided to visit the food trucks that were always parked on the street outside the ME's office. There were picnic tables where she could sit and eat in the sun as she tried to reach her son.

Peggy was in line at the taco food truck when a blue and white police cruiser pulled into the drive.

Paul poked his head out and grinned at her. "What already? I've got like a million texts and voicemails from you and Mai. If you're getting tacos, get three for me. Where's Mai?"

Peggy stared at her son's bright red hair that was cut in a flat top. His laughing green eyes revealed that he thought the whole thing was amusing. She wasn't sure if she should kiss him or hit him.

"Where have you been? All you had to do was answer one of those millions of texts or voice messages, and no one would've bothered you again. Mai isn't eating lunch because she's so worried about you."

Paul's lean face, that reminded her so much of John's, lost its humorous expression. "Is that why you called Al? What's going on? Is she all right? Is Rosie okay?"

"Just park the car, and if you're lucky, I'll get you lunch. But I'll warn you in advance that it comes with an angry mother."

"Okay. I'll go in and see Mai first. Meet you over there at the picnic table. Get her something too. She needs to eat."

Peggy finally reached the tiny window in the taco food truck. She ordered the same thing for all three of them—vegetable tacos with cheese. She didn't waste any time trying to come up with individual food choices. She was impatient to know what was going on.

She could see Mai arguing with Paul all the way out of the building through the front glass panels. The couple met Peggy at the wooden table beneath the sprawling magnolia tree, still fighting.

"I shouldn't even be out here." Mai was yelling at him. "You've compromised my position here. Everything I've worked for could be lost. What were you thinking?"

"If you'd just give me a chance to explain." He tried to reason with her.

Peggy held on to the food and drink boxes. She hoped

they'd finish before the food was ruined.

"Just one thing," Mai said. "Are you or are you not working as a private investigator?"

Paul's green eyes, so much like Peggy's, were deadly serious when he admitted the truth. "Yes. I'm working as a private investigator."

Henbit

Henbit is part of the mint family. Its popular name comes from watching chickens eat it, thus deeming it fit for human consumption during pioneer days. Hummingbirds and honeybees enjoy the tiny purple flowers too. The plant is often used for erosion control and is the first to bloom in the spring.

Chapter Eight

"*What?*"

Both women asked the question at the same time with equal amounts of anger and astonishment.

"I'm sorry." Paul took two tacos and started eating. "I've only got a few minutes, and I'm hungry."

Mai knocked the tacos from his hand to the ground. "And you think you're just going to sit here and eat like nothing's happening? What do you mean you're working as a private investigator? That's completely crazy. When were you planning to tell me?"

Paul faced her wrath. "I figured out last year—when Harry was here—that he could get a lot more done outside the police than I'll ever be able to working in the system."

"Is this about your father?" Peggy asked.

"Yes. In just that short time working with Harry, we learned more about Dad's death—and the circumstances surrounding it—than I had in ten years. Everyone wants to look away from it. Al keeps telling me they'll figure it out.

But they aren't figuring it out—the case file is sitting in lockup somewhere. It's not on anyone's desk. We have no idea what really happened to him."

Mai sighed heavily and handed him one of her tacos. "I understand. But you can't run around telling people you're a private investigator when you work for the police."

He bit into his taco. "It's the best recommendation in the world. People trust me because of it. They're willing to talk to me."

"You know that Steve is looking into your father's death," Peggy reminded him.

Paul grimaced. "No offense to Steve, but how do we know he wasn't involved with Dad's death? We know they were working together, and that he was in love with you."

Peggy was horrified by his statement. "Steve didn't kill your father to get to me. They were working together on something for the FBI. It happens—you know it happens."

"What about the missing file that was taken from the library last year at the house?" he demanded. "Did he ever admit to taking it? He didn't know it wasn't the only copy. He was trying to keep us from knowing what happened to Dad. Why can't you see that?"

"I don't think it's true. Steve wouldn't do that."

He drank half of his soda in a single gulp. "You don't want to see it because you fell for him."

"And you became a private investigator to prove Steve is guilty of some misdoing with your father?" Mai asked. "That's the most stupid thing I've ever heard. What about me? You didn't think about what would happen if something you did as a private investigator ended up on my desk."

Paul wiped his hands on a napkin. "I don't know what you mean. I haven't done much investigating. I've done a few things for extra money, but that's not the point of getting my PI license. I just didn't want to spend any of our money on anything."

"We found your business card at the scene of a murder today," Mai told him. "I have to enter it into evidence. Your friend, Lieutenant McDonald, is going to want to know why it was there."

"Where?" he asked. "What murder?"

"At the condominiums on Providence Road," Peggy told him. "Nita Honohan was found dead this morning."

He appeared stunned by the information. "That's crazy. I didn't do a job for her. That was a simple delivery. It paid well, and it was easy to find her. I gave her my business card at her door. I never even went inside. How did she die?"

"We think she was poisoned by a topical solution that worked like acid on her skin causing her to go into shock," Peggy explained.

"Why were you there?" Mai demanded. "What did you deliver?"

He shrugged. "I delivered a gift in a big box. I don't know what it was. Her friend wanted to surprise her on her birthday. I took the job—it paid a thousand dollars—looked her up, and delivered the package last night."

Mai pushed her silky black hair back from her face. "He's going to be on the video dropping off the mink to her."

Peggy put the food and drink boxes on the ground. "Do you have something from this client who hired you to deliver the box?"

"Hopefully showing something that says she bought it from the fur store and then signed a document saying she wanted you to deliver it," Mai added.

"I only met her once at Providence Cafe. We had coffee, and she gave me the cash. She already had the box. I got it from her and looked up Ms. Honohan to deliver it to her. I already deposited the money in the bank."

"What was her name—the woman who hired you?" Peggy's throat felt so tight that she could hardly speak.

"Her name was Hood. Mary Hood. I've got her cell phone number here somewhere. I don't have an address. What's wrong, Mom? Are you okay?"

Magnolia
The stately magnolia, long considered the epitome of Southern plant life, has been deemed 'messy and possibly not desirable' to assist home sales by real estate agents because of the tree's leaf and fruit litter. Some agents have even gone so far as to advise homeowners to cut down their magnolia trees for faster sales.

Chapter Nine

It was difficult for Peggy to explain what she feared was happening. She couldn't quite make sense of it in her own mind.

What was it anyway? A woman named Mary Hood pretending to hire Sam to work at her house and then hiring Paul to deliver a lethal mink coat.

What did it mean?

When she'd finished telling Mai and Paul everything, the three of them sat on the bench saying nothing for a few minutes as birds called above them in the magnolia and city traffic raced by on the street.

"I'll turn myself in," Paul said.

"You haven't done anything wrong." Mai dabbed at her eyes with a tissue.

He smiled at her and took her hand. "You have to turn in my business card as evidence in this case. I'll be on that video going into the lobby with the box that held the coat and asking for her. The only chance I have is to explain my side of the story right away. The sooner I do that, the more favorably they'll look at it."

"I agree with you, Paul." Peggy's heart was aching with the necessity of him making this decision.

"I can wait and send all the evidence together at five p.m.," Mai said. "That way Peggy has time to work on the rest of her theory about the plant matter that killed Ms. Honohan."

"That's not going to look good for me either," Paul said. "My mother is not only a forensic botanist, but one of the leading botanists in her field researching plant poison."

Peggy put her hand on his arm. "I know. That thought crossed my mind. I'm so sorry."

"For what? Because I put myself in this position? If I wouldn't have wanted to play detective, I wouldn't have delivered that box. We wouldn't be having this conversation."

Mai hugged him tightly. "I love you. Yes, you were stupid to think you could do this without anyone knowing, but your heart was in the right place."

"We'll figure this out," Peggy promised. "I don't know why this is happening, but we'll get to the bottom of it."

Paul hugged her. "I know. I've got to get back. Thanks for the tacos."

He and Mai shared a passionate kiss before he got back in the cruiser and left the parking lot.

"Do you get the feeling that someone has it in for you?" Mai asked as they watched him leave.

"The thought has occurred to me. It's crazy, but we can't ignore it."

"We can't prove it either."

The walked into the ME's office together, each going in separate directions.

Peggy went back to the lab to isolate as many plant

compounds as she could find in the sample they'd taken. It was hard to focus on her work with so much going on.

Was this really about her? She could see why Mai would think that—the shop, Sam's misdirected job, and now Paul.

Maybe it was all part of some grand scheme, but it could also be random acts that only appeared to be part of the same thing.

Her mind ran around in circles as she searched for answers.

By five p.m., she had listed the poisons that were in the sample. The two biggest compounds were from giant hogweed and a mixture of sumac, oak, and ivy. Together they were a volatile poison.

"So you think this was what killed our victim?" Mai asked in her most professional voice.

"Yes, I do. The reaction to giant hogweed alone would've been dramatic and life threatening. Someone managed to make the mixture much stronger than just the normal sap from the plant, and that's powerful enough. Adding these other poisons made it deadly."

Mai handed her the standard medical examiner's form. "If you could sign off here, that will be our official word on it. Thanks for working so quickly."

"Have you heard from Paul?" Peggy signed the sheet.

"No, not yet. I was trying to get all our evidence together. When I turn it in, I hope to get a look at what else they have. We know Paul's prints are on the box. We couldn't get any prints from the mink. Let's hope there's something else that the police picked up from Ms. Honohan's neighbors that will subtract from Paul's involvement."

"Let me know if anything changes. I'll see you later, Mai."

Peggy put away her white coat and picked up her handbag. Feeling like a zombie, she walked out of the building after saying goodnight to the guard at the entrance and got in her car to go home.

There were two calls on her phone. One was from Eve Malcolm, and the other was from Bobby Dean. Both calls pertained to The Potting Shed when all she wanted to do was think about Paul and a way to help him get out of the situation he was in.

She took a moment to compose her thoughts and called Eve.

"We have a few questions about the vandalism, Peggy. Could you come to the office? We can talk about everything here."

"Sure. I'll be there in a few minutes. Thanks for calling."

Peggy decided to wait to return Bobby's call until after she spoke with Eve. There might be information that would help her get through the rest of the process to receive her reimbursement.

Eve worked in the same building where John had worked. Even though it had been more than ten years since his death, almost everything looked the same. New people came in, and old people left, but the furniture and surroundings didn't change. Al's office was here too.

And she could never resist a peek at the person in John's old office.

Peggy went inside the brick building. She knew the sergeant at the front desk. He told her he'd call Sergeant Malcolm.

While she waited, she took the dead leaves off a heart-leaf philodendron near the small window beside the door. The constant change of cold and hot air had stunted the growth of the plant, leaving the leaves very tiny, but otherwise it was healthy.

Eve saw her. "Thanks for coming by. Come on back."

Peggy glanced around at the busy police officers. She wondered if Paul was being questioned somewhere in the building. Would Al stay on the case, or would he recuse himself because of their relationship?

"Take a seat, please." Eve closed the door to the room where she'd led her.

It wasn't Eve's office, as she would have expected on this visit. It was a small interrogation room.

Peggy's heart rate went up. "Is there a problem?"

Eve sat opposite her at the new metal table complete with a metal bar to lock handcuffs to. "I'm not going to lie to you or sugarcoat the situation. Homicide is looking at your son, Paul, for Ms. Nita Honohan's murder. It complicates matters for us that the break-in at your shop happened around the same time."

"I'm not sure I follow."

"I have the list of plants that were destroyed in the break-in at your shop, but there is no mention of the giant hog wart on that list. Isn't that what killed Ms. Honohan?"

Peggy smiled. "Giant hogweed. Sorry."

Eve nodded. "Our question, Peggy, is whether or not you had the components for this lethal plant mixture at your shop?"

"Of course not! No one would want to plant hogweed, poison ivy, oak, or sumac in their yards. That would be ridiculous. Garden shops don't deal in weeds. Besides, you could get the last three ingredients in any forest around here. The hogweed doesn't grow here yet, but you could get that in Virginia. Why would I have that at The Potting Shed?"

"Homicide believes Paul may have obtained the poison plants from you. It's what you're known for, isn't it—your specialty. It's what makes you valuable as a forensic botanist with the ME's office, right?"

"It is what I'm known for," she agreed. "But I have never stored poisonous plants in the shop."

Eve tucked a strand of black hair behind her ear as she looked at a list on the desk. "What about hellebore, rhododendron, or lilies? Those are poisonous, aren't they?"

"If you want to look at it that way, dozens of plants you grow in your house and yard could be used to make poison. Most people don't know that and wouldn't know what to do with the information if they did."

"But a man was found dead in your shop several years ago after being poisoned with anemone, right?"

"Yes, but he wasn't poisoned with anemone bulbs from my shop. Can you be more specific? What makes you think that I'd help someone, even my own son, poison this woman? I've always made it very clear that I won't help anyone when they ask about poison plants."

Peggy knew, at least partially, that this line of questioning came from the police looking for answers about the murder. She didn't like it, but she had to remain calm and answer as precisely as she could.

She wasn't sure who'd given Eve the plant names. She could tell by the way she read the list that she had no idea what she was talking about. She could've simply looked it up on Google. Maybe she was being paranoid, thinking another plant authority could be involved.

But after the day she'd had, Peggy felt entitled to be a bit paranoid.

"The nature of this crime, and your son being involved, makes this difficult for me. We all thought at first that this was a simple, though devastating, vandalism at your shop. Now Captain Hager has taken over the homicide investigation. He believes this break-in is probably personal—that it's likely that Paul broke into your shop and vandalized it to cover his tracks."

"No."

"You received a new shipment of plants the day before

the break-in, is that right?"

Eve kept glancing at the mirror on the wall. Captain Hager was probably watching. This had gone from small potatoes to something much larger in a day.

"Yes. I believe my assistant emailed you the list of plants that we'd received."

Eve nodded. "I have that shipping order here. It was convenient that there was no real buyer for the plants, no paper trail of exactly who paid for these plants or why they were ordered."

"Convenient? Certainly not for me. To begin with, the company we order from wouldn't carry hogweed or poison oak in stock." She stared into the mirror. "If you knew anything about plants at all, you wouldn't ask me these questions."

"But you admit that Paul could have added to the order Sam made and then destroyed everything that arrived except for what he needed to cover up the murder." Eve pushed her ideas behind the conversation.

Peggy took a deep breath. Her fiery red hair might have begun going white, but she still had a temper. "I don't admit that at all. Weeks go by that Paul doesn't even visit The Potting Shed. And though I love him dearly, he wouldn't know the difference between a raspberry bush and a grapevine. He's not a gardener."

Eve leaned forward, her black eyes intent on Peggy's face. "I've been to The Potting Shed many times, Peggy. I know Selena keeps the laptop on the counter. Wouldn't it be possible for Paul to get into the shop and change the order before it was sent out?"

"No. The gardening supply company wouldn't send poisonous plants in their shipment, and Paul wouldn't know what to ask for. This line of questioning isn't going to get you anywhere, Eve."

"Yet you admitted that this supply company has sent you other poisonous plants in the past."

"I guess I can't explain the difference between an ornamental, potentially poisonous plant such as Easter lilies, and a deadly one like hogweed if you know nothing about plants. If you're going to pursue this, you need an advisor who can tell you the difference." Peggy got to her feet and faced the mirror. "And that's not going to be me. If I'm not under arrest, I'm leaving now."

"I'm sorry this has happened, Peggy." Eve she stood too. "It's a difficult situation. I know it must be painful for you."

"Not painful at all, Eve. It's ridiculous. I'll talk to you later."

Poison Ivy
Not to be confused with English ivy. In 1784, Philadelphia horticulturalist William Bartram sent seeds for poison ivy and sumac home to be used in the United States as garden plants. So the next time you run into a poison ivy plant and are enduring the following rash you know who to thank!

Chapter Ten

Captain Avery Hager was waiting for Peggy when she left the interrogation room.

He nodded to Eve, and she introduced him.

"Dr. Lee. I'll be taking over this case for Lieutenant McDonald." He smiled pleasantly. "I'm sorry to meet you under these circumstances. I've been to many of your seminars."

"Captain Hager." Peggy wasn't surprised to learn that Al had been removed from the case since their families were so close.

"I want you to know that it doesn't give me any pleasure to put you through this, Dr. Lee. And I'm sorry about your son. He has an unblemished record with the department."

Her green eyes flashed her anger. "But none of that matters because you have this crazy notion that Paul killed this woman."

He nodded. "Good men go bad sometimes."

"If my son has gone bad," she questioned, "what was his motive? I know you don't think he killed her for a thousand dollars. What's the thinking behind the murder?"

"I'm afraid I'm not at liberty to discuss that with you, Dr. Lee."

"Cop speak for you don't know. I was married to your predecessor. I know the lingo."

"It would be best for all of us if your son confessed. I'm sure with his record, the DA would offer some kind of deal. You should talk to him. Don't let these circumstances drag your family's name through the mud."

"I'll certainly see what I can do to prevent that, Captain Hager. Thanks for your help."

Peggy held her head high and her back straight as she stormed out of the police station. Her feet were quick on the stairs as she wondered where Paul was. Obviously, he hadn't been charged. They didn't have enough evidence.

Al was waiting in the parking lot for her. "Rough day, huh?"

"A horrible day." She leaned against the car beside him. "I'm ready to wake up now. This has to be a nightmare."

He put his big arm around her. "Me too. I'm not suspended, but I can't go near Paul's case."

"I understand. Don't feel bad about it. We'll figure it out."

"I already told Mary that I'm taking some vacation time. They can keep me from looking into the facts of this case on the department's time but not on my own."

Peggy studied his broad, brown face that was so dear to her. "Don't get yourself in trouble too. We'll handle it."

"Excuse me—who is the senior police officer in this family? If this had happened to Mary, and John was alive, he'd do exactly what I'm going to do. We'll figure it out, but that includes me."

She hugged him, tears misting her eyes. "Thank you."

"Where are you off to now?"

"I need to call the insurance adjuster and let Sam and Selena know what's going on. Steve is out of town tomorrow yet. Do you know where Paul went?"

"I know he was assigned to desk duty after they questioned him. That's standard procedure as they work the investigation. I assumed he might be home with Mai and the baby."

Peggy decided to go home. She let all their close friends and family know that she was holding a meeting at the house. She needed everyone to be in the loop until they could make sense of this.

Al followed her after a quick call to his wife, Mary. Sam brought Selena. Paul and Mai came a few minutes later with Baby Rosie.

"The insurance adjuster said his investigation of the break-in and vandalism couldn't be concluded until the police investigation is over," Peggy told them. She'd talked to Bobby Dean who was very sorry to hold up the money she needed to restock The Potting Shed, but his hands were tied.

"I'm still gonna get that shipment," Sam said. "It will be here first thing tomorrow, and we'll have to pay for it. I don't know where we should store it since there's no alarm and the police might have to go through the shop again. I've sold about twenty five hundred dollars of it so far. Any ideas?"

"Divert it here," Peggy decided. "Call them right now and have it brought here. If necessary, we can cover some of it with tarps, but it will probably be fine out in the yard."

"Good idea," Al added. "The police might want to look through it for poisonous plants. Captain Hager is convinced that's where Paul got the hogweed."

"From a garden supply company?" Sam snorted.

"Seriously?"

"They don't know much about plants," Al said. "That's why we hire Peggy when the need arises."

"Like I'd know what hogweed looks like," Paul said. "But whoever set this up knew that my mother knows all about poison plants."

"Mary Hood," Sam said the name. "It's what we're all thinking, right? For whatever reason, Mary Hood has made it her occupation to ruin our lives. That's what I think anyway."

Selena shrugged. "It makes sense to me. The vandalism shut down The Potting Shed. This whole thing, with an unknown woman pretending to be Mary Hood, is just bad for business. And Mary Hood framed Paul for murder."

"That's a stretch, little girl," Al said. "We have no proof of any of that."

"And yet it happened," Paul reminded him. "This can't be coincidence."

There was a knock on the kitchen door that Shakespeare responded to, glad to have a chance to run for it. Peggy answered and found Millie waiting there with Hunter.

"Anyone call for a lawyer?" Hunter asked with a grin.

"I might know a few people who need one," Peggy responded with a smile. "Come on inside and join the party."

It was getting late. Peggy ordered pizza for her group of strategists. They'd spread out in the dining room around the big antique oak table as they planned their next move.

"We should definitely pay a visit to Stewart's Fur Shop," Al said. "Hager has the box and the coat. He'll try to get the information for the customer who sent it to Nita Honohan. They'll be focused on Paul's name and credit card information. We need to take a look at everything the shop has for that day. I'm thinking Mary Hood's name isn't on that list, but someone else who bought one of those minks is."

"What will we do when we get the information?" Selena asked. "We can't arrest anyone."

"No," Sam agreed. "But we can step on them."

Paul and Al both frowned at him.

"What? Maybe this is someone trying to get to Peggy, but my part of the business is hurt by it too, and I'm out there selling my ass off to make up for what this person did."

"Are you sure there was no one with this woman who ordered plants from you?" Millie asked in a quiet voice.

"No. We were completely alone. It's not unusual. Most of the bank executives and other professional husbands aren't interested in what their wives do with the house and yard. Even my best clients—I've never met their husbands. The wives have the check books."

"What about this fake Mary Hood?" Millie wrote down his response in her notebook. "What did she look like? Do you think you could describe her for a sketch artist?"

Sam shrugged. "Sure."

"But we don't have a sketch artist," Mai said.

"Maybe I could help with that." Selena raised her hand. "I've taken art for the last two years. I'm not Rembrandt, but I could do a crude sketch that would give us an idea of who we're dealing with."

"Great idea," Millie said. "Anybody got paper?"

"There should be some in the library." Paul got to his feet.

Peggy paid the pizza delivery guy at the door. Shakespeare's big head almost knocked the pizza box out of her hands as she turned around. Her cell phone rang, and she put the boxes on the kitchen table.

"Peggy? It's Dorothy Beck. They've called me back from the seminar, can you believe it? I can't even get away for two days."

They both laughed at that, but it was a forced response. Both women knew why she was calling.

"I'm sorry, Peggy, but you can't work on the Honohan case anymore. Conflict of interest. You know. I have to call Mai as well. You're both on leave until this is over. I wish it could be different."

Ferns
These plants reproduce by spores but possess true roots, stems, and complex leaves. These are ancient plants, dating back millions of years, and there are about 12,000 species. We may never know exactly how many species there are because some are lost every day to development in rain forests.

Chapter Eleven

It wasn't totally a surprise that Dr. Beck had to pull them from the team.

Mai was emotional—she had more to lose than Peggy—and had to leave the room for a few minutes while everyone else ate pizza.

"I guess it goes along with taking me off the case," Al said. "This pizza is good. Where did it come from?"

"Giovanni's." Peggy didn't feel much like eating either. Working for the ME's office wasn't her entire livelihood as it was for Mai. She didn't have expectations of moving up the ladder as her daughter-in-law did. Mai had hopes of someday taking Dr. Beck's place.

Still, it was a black mark on her reputation. To be accused of working with Paul to kill Nita Honohan was enough to close all doors to her working with other botanists around the world. They needed a viable answer that would take the blame away from Paul. That would change everything back to the way it was. That was what she had to focus on for all their sakes.

They put Selena in the dining room with paper and pencil, away from the pizza and conversation. Millie sent Sam in first to make sure his description of Mary Hood wasn't tainted by Paul's description.

Peggy called Walter to let him know that there would be a noisy early morning delivery the next day. She didn't answer his questions, telling him she had company at her house.

"If this woman has a criminal background, we should be able to ID her in the FBI database." Millie carefully made sure her lipstick wasn't smeared by the pizza.

"She must have some knowledge of botany," Hunter said. "Otherwise how could she know to use this hogweed poison?"

"You could pick it up from Google," Peggy answered. "I'm afraid making botanical poison isn't that difficult. If you have a rudimentary intelligence, you could figure it out. It's gruesome. I wouldn't have thought of it as a way to kill someone. And I hope other people who read about it don't try it."

Mai came back in the kitchen as Selena was done working with Sam on the sketch.

"I'm sorry. I guess I just lost it."

"Don't worry about it." Al squeezed her shoulder. "You just take care of you and that baby. Let us do this."

Mai pushed herself up to her full height and faced him proudly. "I have twelve years' experience with the medical examiner's office. I can be a valuable member of this team. And since I have more to lose than anyone else here, I plan to take care of Rosie and make sure Paul doesn't end up in prison."

Al held up his hands in surrender. "You are absolutely right. I apologize."

Sam grabbed some pizza. "Don't ask me about the sketch. Millie says I shouldn't talk about it."

Millie had gone into the dining room with Paul so she could witness the procedure and make sure it was done correctly.

"Good," Hunter said. "That's what we need. Anything less won't hold up in court."

Everyone ate at least one slice of pizza, and Mai fed Rosie. Shakespeare looked so despondently at the empty pizza boxes, that Peggy gave him a dog treat. He carried it into the other part of the house, satisfied.

Conversation lagged as they waited for the outcome of the two sketches. What their next move would be hinged on what Selena drew.

It was a surprise, and a disappointment, when the two versions of Mary Hood didn't match.

"How's that possible?" Sam asked. "There are two women named Mary Hood living in Charlotte and trying to ruin our lives? I don't believe it."

Selena held up the sketch she'd done of Sam's version of Mary Hood. She had long brown hair and had been wearing sunglasses the whole time because they'd been outside.

Paul's version of the woman had short blond hair and blue eyes.

Peggy stared at both of them. "Let's skip the face and ask another question—how tall was she? Small? Medium? Large? It's hard to hide your height."

"She was pretty short." Sam held his hand at mid-chest level. "Petite, I guess, and thin."

Paul mostly agreed with that. "Not thin. She had large hips and breasts."

"But short, right?" Al asked. "You can add padding and change wigs, but it's hard to hide height."

"So we assume she's short and thin—you can't make yourself thinner—and she probably has short hair," Peggy said. "Maybe she has blue eyes. It's hard to say with contacts."

"What about her age?" Millie asked. "Young? Old? Middle-aged?"

Sam glanced at Paul. "I think fifties. What about you?"

"Late forties or early fifties. She was wearing a lot of make-up."

"Yeah. I'd say that too," Sam agreed.

"It could be the same woman," Mai said. "If you could set up another meeting with her, Paul, I could jab her with a needle and do a DNA test. We'd know who she is soon enough."

Paul put his arm around his wife. "Getting a little vicious, are we? Why not just shoot her?"

Mai hugged Rosie tight. "I'm good with that. She's trying to ruin our lives and doing a good job at it."

"That's not gonna happen," Al said. "We can describe her as a short, thin woman in her late forties or early fifties when we go to Stewart's Furs to have a look at their customer list for the day."

"How are we going to get something like that without a court order?" Hunter asked.

"We don't need a court order," Paul said. "I have my PI license. I can use that as ID."

Mai groaned. "That's what got us into all this trouble."

"I'm sorry," Paul said.

Rosie was tired and started fussing, so Paul and Mai decided to go home. There was nothing more they could do until the next day.

Millie talked with Al before she left. She wanted him to be very careful that he didn't jeopardize his thirty-plus years on the job. "You're only off this case right now," she cautioned. "I'm sure you don't want it to be a permanent thing."

Al laughed. "My wife would shoot you if she thought you were trying to keep me from retiring. I'm not worried about CMPD finding out that I've helped Peggy. I've given them a lot of good years. That includes losing my best friend to the job. If they want to get rid of me for what I do on vacation—so be it."

Millie shrugged. "I understand. I'll see you all later. Hang in there, Peggy. We'll make this right."

Peggy hugged her and said goodbye. Hunter left with Millie. Peggy hadn't realized the two women were friends. She'd only known them to have met a few times at her house.

"We're going too, unless you want me to stay," Sam offered. "I can take Selena home and come back. I don't know if you should be alone."

"I'll be fine. Shakespeare is here, and I lived alone in this house for many years. Don't worry about it. Get some sleep. I know that plant shipment is coming early."

"You won't sleep through it either, you know," Sam joked. "Those guys are noisy, and so is their truck. They aren't used to quiet urban neighborhoods. You might get some angry calls from your neighbors."

"Drop it off in that big open area by the garage. Only Walter will know, and I'll tell him to expect it."

Sam, Selena, and Peggy hugged before they left.

Al was the last to go. "Come and stay with me and Mary until Steve gets back. I know you lived here alone for a long time, but now it isn't the same thing. We don't know what this woman has in mind. If she's masterminded both these events to attack you and your family, she's clever and resourceful. You should be making a list of your enemies."

She smiled and hugged him. "You know I don't have any enemies. And I'll be fine until Steve gets back. I'll set the alarm and probably spend the night in the basement with my plants. Whatever this woman has in store, she must not want to kill me, just ruin my life. And we don't even know that for sure yet."

"Okay. If you're sure I can't change your mind." He squeezed her hand. "Call me if you need anything—I mean anything. Don't wait for it to be life-threatening. We don't know for sure Mary Hood *isn't* out there waiting to kill you either."

Al finally left. Peggy fed Shakespeare and then made sure all the doors were locked. He gobbled his food down quickly and quietly followed her to each door.

She set the outer perimeter alarm and turned off the lights upstairs. Shakespeare followed her into the basement to sniff the sliding glass doors and whine as though asking if she'd made sure those doors were locked too.

"They're always locked," she told him. "Unless you're asking to go out. Is that it?"

In answer, he walked around in a circle on his rug and then collapsed on it. He whined and beat his tail on the floor once or twice before laying his head down and closing his eyes.

Peggy patted his head and gave him a kiss. "I guess that means you don't want to go out. But you know how boring it is for you being down here so you're taking a nap. Good choice."

She hadn't exaggerated about staying in the basement. She'd put in a cot and a small fridge years ago. Sometimes when she was working on a project that needed to be checked every twenty minutes, it was easier to stay down here.

It hadn't happened as much since she'd married Steve. She tended to limit those time-consuming projects, but that didn't stop her from being a member of several botanical groups that did research into various types of plants.

She really loved working with groups that were looking for ways to make food plants go further. She'd grown large tomatoes—the size of soccer balls—and fast-growing short wheat that took less time and space to produce a full harvest.

Peggy liked working on ornamental hybrids too. She'd produced the first night blooming rose, dozens of miniature lilies, and huge ferns.

She checked each of her experiments every day and kept records of their growth rates and variables of temperature and humidity as well as any problems she encountered.

Currently she was working on a project with twelve other botanists from around the world to prove if melatonin enhanced growth in soybeans. So far her findings had been good. Her soybeans had grown more energetically and abundantly than soybeans grown without melatonin.

With the basement running the entire length of the big house, and every inch of the ceiling covered with grow lights, she had a big project at the far end. Enhanced spinach, the size of ten-foot elephant ears, was growing. Normal spinach was packed with vitamins and iron. One leaf of her spinach held enough vitamins and iron for an entire day.

She was thrilled with the thick, dark green leaves and enormous stems. They didn't require good soil either, which was always a plus for growers. And the taste was excellent. She picked off a small leaf and chewed it as she went to check on her other plants.

In the heart of the basement was a small pond where she worked on the dwarf cattails, irises, and other water plants before she took them to The Potting Shed to sell. She also had some lovely water lilies that always made her day better just looking at them.

She cupped one of the large floating yellow lilies with her hands and smiled. They were so beautiful. It was hard to maintain any anger or frustration when she was down here with her babies.

Peggy was getting ready to check on her peanuts that could remove food allergies from other peanut plants and foods derived from them. The doorbell rang upstairs. She jumped nervously, and for the first time since Steve had the unit installed, she turned on the monitor that could show her who was at the door.

"Hi, honey." Her father and mother waved to her. "Sam gave us a call and told us about what's happening. We've brought a few things so we can stay here with you until Steve comes back."

Cotton
No one knows exactly how old cotton is. Cotton bolls and cloth have been found in Mexico that are at least 7,000 years old. Cotton has changed very little from what is grown today. Colonists in America were growing cotton in 1616 along the James River in Virginia, creating a whole new, wealthier way of life for many.

Chapter Twelve

Like many people, Peggy had a love-hate relationship with her family.

She got along better with her father, Ranson Hughes, than she did her mother, Lilla. She was more like her father in personality but more like her mother in looks. She got her red hair from her mother and unfortunately, her short body, prone to gain weight by looking at a slice of cake.

Ranson was tall and thin with a patient disposition. He didn't like to stir things up the way Peggy and her mother did. Most of the time, he got between them when there was trouble.

Peggy went upstairs with Shakespeare at her heels. They went to the kitchen door and opened it for her parents—a big hug from her father and polite air kisses from her mother.

"Why didn't you call us?" Lilla demanded as Ranson maneuvered their suitcases into the house.

"She didn't want to bother us," her father said. "Don't

pick at her now. She's had a rough day. We're not here to make it worse."

"What about Paul's job?" Lilla continued as she strode confidently into the house leaving her handbag on the kitchen table with her pink sweater. "Is he going to be all right? I can't believe you didn't at least tell us about this. He's our grandson, and Rosie is our great-granddaughter. We have a right to know."

"Everything happened so quickly," Peggy began to explain. "I didn't think of it. I'm sorry."

"That's okay, honey." Ranson smiled. "Where should I put these bags?"

"You really don't have to stay with me. Steve is only gone one more night. I'll be fine." *And I'm going to kick Sam for calling you as soon as I see him.*

"We're here now, Margaret," her father said.

"And we're not going home until things get better," her mother added imperiously.

Peggy sighed. "Follow me."

They walked through the rambling old house that had been built during the turn of the last century for John's family. It was big, even compared to the other large houses around it.

Situated on an acre of land in the heart of Myer's Park, the house had dozens of bedrooms, a large library, and a dining room that could easily seat twenty. The Lee family had made their money from shipping, and this was where John's great-great-grandfather had brought his new bride.

Everything in the building of the house had been carefully chosen and selected to last a lifetime. Hardwood floors and paneled walls had been cut in Wilmington and brought to Charlotte. Expensive chandeliers and furniture were the best money could buy at the time.

Peggy had been raised in Charleston, South Carolina as

the only child of a gentleman farmer on hundreds of acres of land close to the sea. But she'd lost her heart to John Lee when they were in college, and it was here that he'd brought her as well.

John had inherited the house and land as part of a legacy. Paul didn't inherit it at John's death. The trust went to John's nephew, who wasn't ready to settle down.

She lived there with his good graces but without the elder family members' approval. They were even unhappier when she'd married Steve, but it was important for someone to live in the house. She loved the old place and thought it might as well be her.

They walked through the ground floor past the thirty-two foot blue spruce that was growing under the skylight beside the circular staircase. Peggy had planted that right after she and John had moved here. She felt as though it was the soul of the house.

Her mother and father followed her up the three-story marble staircase. Peggy loved its cool smoothness beneath her bare feet in the summer. Shakespeare had a hard time with it, slipping and sliding down the stairs more often than walking down.

Peggy put her mother and father in the blue suite next to her room. Everything was done in shades of blue as it had been when she'd moved there—minus the moth-eaten drapes and bedclothes. The previous heir hadn't been very interested in upgrading things in or around the grand old estate.

"The bathroom is in there." She pointed. "You know the rest of the house. You can stay here as long as you like. You know the invitation is always open."

Ranson put the luggage on the bed. "Was that pizza I smelled downstairs? I'm starving. What about you, Lilla?"

"I'm exhausted from packing and worrying about my family." She sat in the large velvet chair beside the window that overlooked Queens Road. "And you shouldn't eat pizza."

"There are a few slices left," Peggy told her father. "I can reheat them if you'd like."

He smiled. "You know I like it better cold, little girl. Come down and sit with me anyway. Let your mother get some rest."

Peggy and her mother hugged briefly, not too tight or close.

"If you need anything, Mom, let me know. There are clean towels in the closet at the end of the hall. I'll see you in the morning."

"Yes. And we'll talk about what you're doing to make this right. Goodnight, Margaret."

Ranson and Shakespeare went down first. Peggy followed them. She hoped Shakespeare wouldn't knock her father down the stairs. But they managed to make it to the bottom safely.

Her mother and father had moved to Charlotte a few years back after selling their farm. They'd wanted to be close to her, to Paul, and the new baby, finally realizing that she was never moving back home again. They had a small house between Paul and Peggy's places that made it convenient to see them regularly.

She put the cold pizza out on the table for her father, found a beer in the back of the refrigerator and put that out too. Father and daughter sat at the same wood table that John had used as a child with his mother and father.

"So, Sam was a little short on explaining what happened to Paul. I think I understand the whole thing about him getting bamboozled by some pretty girl into doing something that may have caused someone else's death. Is that about right?"

Peggy opened the bottle of beer as her father chewed his pizza. "Something like that. Paul is working as a private detective and got caught in the middle of a murder. That's about all we know right now."

Ranson's gray brows went up in his lean face. "You mean like *Rockford Files*? We used to love that show. Did they already fire him from the police department?"

"No. He hasn't been fired. He was working on the side to try to figure out what happened to John. You know he's always wanted to do that."

"I know. He's been like a bear with a honeycomb stuck on his paw. We've talked about it a few times. I think he would've been better off hiring a private detective than becoming one. Lilla and I would've been glad to foot the bill if the Lee family isn't interested."

"It's not that they aren't interested. They believe what the police said. Paul and I have learned better."

Ranson quickly polished off a slice of cheese pizza and took a few sips of beer. "He's got a family now, Margaret. He can't go off on these wild hares looking for what happened to his daddy. He has to consider his daughter and Mai."

"I know. I had no idea what he was doing."

"He lives close by." Ranson chuckled. "You're not up in his business enough. That's what mothers are for. Ask Lilla if you don't believe me."

"If we can get him out of this mess with his job intact, I'm sure it will be a while before Paul uses his PI license again."

"And can you get him out of this?"

Peggy frowned. "I hope so, Dad."

Spiraea
Sometimes considered to be a pest, spiraea shrubs are in the Rosacea family and have been known as medicinal plants for hundreds of years. The shrubs contain salicylates, such as those found in aspirin, and may have been the first source of the drug.

Chapter Thirteen

Peggy and her father talked in the kitchen until her mother yelled over the rail upstairs that it was time to go to bed. They separated with a hug, and Peggy curled up with Shakespeare for the night in her bed.

It seemed as though she'd just gone to sleep when she heard loud banging and conversation outside. She glanced at the clock on her bedside table. It was five a.m., just barely starting to get light. She'd forgotten how early deliveries came since Sam had taken over that part of the business.

Yawning, she dressed quickly in jeans and a Potting Shed T-shirt. After looking at her red-rimmed green eyes in the bathroom mirror and pulling a brush through her hair, she let Shakespeare out in the backyard. He put his huge paws on top of the wood fence and stared at the people delivering plants, but didn't bark.

Sam was outside in the chilly morning air directing where the plant shipment should go. All the shrubs were set together. All the bulb plants were separated from the others.

Peggy was happy to see that he had a good relationship with the delivery men as he joked with them and put his muscles to use helping them with their task.

She was lucky to have found Sam, even though it was at the cost of his medical career. His parents had always pushed him to be a surgeon as they had pushed Hunter to be a lawyer. They were unhappy with their son's choice of profession and had frequently let him know it. They'd also said a few words to her since they blamed her for Sam's change of heart.

"How do you get them to come so early?" she yawned as she spoke to him.

"They like me. I work with them, and I give them gifts at Christmas."

"Are you sure coming at this hour of the morning means they like you?"

He grinned as he put his arm around her shoulders. "Is this sour grapes because I called Lilla and Ranson last night?"

"That's right. In my near unconscious state, I almost forgot. Later today we'll have words."

When everything was unloaded, Sam left, and Peggy got Shakespeare and went back inside. She'd forgotten to lock the door and set the perimeter alarm while she'd been outside with Sam. She remedied that situation with a touch of the keypad.

She wanted to go back to sleep for an hour or so. She hadn't slept well, nightmares plaguing her dreams. *Not surprising.*

She lay down on the bed but was wide awake. She wasn't exactly sure what the plan was for today. Without her forensic work, and with the shop still closed, it seemed her time was open ended.

Peggy went quietly down the marble stairs again and into the kitchen to make some tea. The kettle was just starting to boil when the kitchen door suddenly opened. She panicked for a moment, grabbing the first thing she saw—an iron frying pan. It would've been better to have a gun, but the frying pan was closer.

Shakespeare lifted his head and started barking, but he was also wagging his tail and moving to the door in a welcoming manner. Peggy knew whoever had a key was someone familiar to him.

"Good morning," Steve said as he turned off the alarm. "I hope I didn't wake you. What's with all the plants in the yard?"

Peggy put down the frying pan and hugged him tightly. "You came home early. Everything was fine. You could've stayed for the whole conference."

He kissed her. "With all the excitement going on here? I didn't want to miss a thing."

They sat at the old wood table together, talking and drinking coffee and tea. She told him all the news as he rubbed Shakespeare's head.

"You've been busy," he said with a smile. "I'm sorry about Paul and your job. I'm sure we can find out who's really behind this, and everything will go back to normal."

"I hope so. And I hope it happens before Paul is formally charged. Right now he's just a person of interest. They've got him as far as delivering the mink coat, and I'm sure they think he knew how to poison it because of me. The one thing they don't have is motive. They can't prove he knew Ms. Honohan before that day. That's the only thing in his favor."

"I agree with Millie that someone is setting you up. Whoever it is has been careful and methodical about what they've done. It wouldn't surprise me for the police to find more evidence to convict Paul."

Peggy shivered as she wrapped her hands around her mug of tea. "But who would do such a thing? If someone set this up, they have to know me very well. They know destroying the store is like ripping out my heart and they knew how to scam Sam into ordering those plants. They want to ruin my reputation and hurt Mai and Paul. I can't think of anyone who's that diabolical."

Steve put his hand over hers. "You should get a pen and paper and think of all the people your personal sleuthing, and working with the ME's office has put in jail. The chances are that's where we'll find the killer."

"Which then would also have to be someone who is out of jail now," she added.

"Exactly. You come up with the list. I'll check it out."

"But you can't be involved," she reminded him. "The FBI wouldn't be part of this."

"If you think I'm going to sit around while this happens to you and Paul, you're wrong. Al has friends too. Between us, we'll get this person, Peggy. Try not to worry about it."

She went downstairs to the basement to check on her work as Steve showered and changed clothes. By the time she got back upstairs, the strong smell of bacon and toast was wafting through the air.

It had to be her father. Her mother rarely cooked—especially not breakfast.

Peggy wasn't surprised to see Ranson cooking a breakfast big enough to feed an army. She was surprised to see Sam and Millie there again.

Steve's assistant, Norris Rankin, was also there. For some reason, Peggy could never find his good side. The two of them butted heads over everything. Sometimes she wondered if he was jealous of her and Steve. It was complicated.

"Good morning, everyone." She smiled at the three people sitting at the table—Norris with his ever-present laptop. "Dad, that's probably enough food for us and all the neighbors."

"It's not as much as it looks," he countered. "Paul is on his way over too. People who eat a good breakfast are happier and more satisfied with their lives. Did you know that? I read it online a few days ago. Get some plates out. I already put on another pot of coffee."

Peggy fed Shakespeare as Al and Paul arrived. Mai had gone into work that day. Dr. Beck planned for her to be on other cases.

Everyone was filling their plates with pancakes, bacon, eggs, and toast as Shakespeare started barking in his way that let her know someone he didn't recognize was outside. She looked out the door and saw several CMPD squad cars in her drive along with a crime scene unit.

"What now?" she asked.

Mock Orange
Also known as orange jasmine. The shrubs exude a citrusy scent, hence the name, but are not related to the orange tree. The plants attract butterflies, which make them popular with gardeners. They can become easily overgrown and must be heartily pruned, which make them less popular.

Chapter Fourteen

Peggy and Steve went outside together with Ranson right behind them. Captain Hager was instructing his officers how to look through the hundreds of plants in containers.

"Why are you here?" Peggy asked him bluntly. She was tired of being nice about it.

"Dr. Lee." He nodded to Steve. "And you are?"

"I'm Agent Steve Newsome, FBI Director for this area—and Dr. Lee's husband. I hope you have a search warrant."

Captain Hager looked momentarily taken aback when Steve introduced himself, but he recovered quickly as he brought out the warrant with a flourish.

"Agent Newsome. I'm assuming you're not here to look into this case."

"No. What are you hoping to find this morning?"

Peggy had been studying the search warrant—she'd seen a lot of them in her day. "He's here because he thinks there might be hogweed plants in this shipment."

"That's right," Captain Hager acknowledged. "Don't play with me. You're trying to hide these plants here instead of taking them to your garden shop. Why is that?"

"Because someone broke into my shop and trashed everything I had. I don't want that to happen again. These plants might not look like much to you, but they're worth ten thousand dollars. We've already lost them once. We can't afford to lose them again."

Sam had joined them outside. "Do you really think there's going to be giant hogweed plants in here? It wouldn't hurt you to do a little homework on this and realize that hogweed is, as its name implies, a weed. You can't buy it as far as I know."

"Excuse us if we want to check that for ourselves." Captain Hager smiled and walked away.

"I've got my Louisville slugger in the car," Ranson growled with his fists clenched.

"Maybe you should go back inside, Dad," Peggy suggested. Paul and Al had wisely stayed in the house. No reason to reveal their plans to find the truth to Hager.

"Good morning," Walter said cheerfully as he approached the group. "I think it's going to be another lovely day."

Captain Hager grunted when he saw him. "Are you Dr. Bellows? Feel free to dive right in."

Peggy was surprised at that. "You told them the plants were being delivered here this morning?"

He shrugged. "I'm so sorry, but it was part of my duty as the forensic botanist on this case to alert them. I knew you wouldn't have hogweed out here. You were completely safe."

Sam took a menacing step toward him, towering over the short man. "You called the cops? I thought you were

Peggy's friend."

Walter took a few steps back. "As I said, I was only observing my due diligence to the city and county by alerting them to the delivery. Anyone in my position would have done the same. Back me up here, Peggy."

"You're on your own," she said. "This was beyond due diligence."

"Why you little weasel—" Sam started after him.

"I'd better go help the police." Walter walked quickly away from them.

"Did you know he took your place with the medical examiner?" Sam asked.

"No," Peggy said. "But since they took me off the case, they were bound to look for another botanist."

"I don't think reporting you to the police is something a friend would do," Ranson said. "I'm going back in. All this has upset my digestion."

Peggy and Sam stayed outside with the police to make sure the plants weren't harmed. A few broken stalks could kill parts of the more delicate plants. Steve went back in with Ranson.

Hunter arrived only a few minutes later, driving her blue Camaro like a demon, which had earned her several speeding tickets since she'd purchased it.

"Let me take a look at that search warrant," she demanded.

"I think it's in order." Peggy gave it to her.

"I'm the lawyer. I'm supposed to decide that stuff. Lucky Sam called me right away. This borders on harassment."

"Not to mention being flat in the middle of stupidity," Sam spat out.

"We're just protecting our investment right now," Peggy said. "If the search warrant is bad, by all means stop them from looking at the plants."

Hunter checked the warrant. "I guess it's okay. But I'm

going to have a word with the lead investigator. Excuse me."

Several of the shrubs were knocked over, top heavy in their pots. There were a few broken branches on the tender young trees too, but otherwise the shipment was fine after the search.

"We're leaving for now," Captain Hager told Peggy. "Dr. Bellows said there is no hogweed here. I guess we'll take his word for it."

Sam growled again as he left them. "I don't understand why they refuse to educate themselves in this matter when Paul's life is on the line."

"Never mind now. It's over. The plants are okay. Do you have somewhere to take them today?"

"Not all of them, but a good number. I had to discount some, but better less money than no money."

"I agree," she said. "Any other thoughts about Mary Hood last night?"

"Not really. I keep going over it in my head, but I've done the same thing a hundred times. I talk to someone, and if we click, they hire me for the job. There was nothing about her that was unusual. She was just another landscaping client."

Peggy patted his large, muscular arm. "Don't drive yourself crazy with it, Sam. You do a good job. There was no way to know you were blindsided."

"It won't happen again," he promised. "I'm taking my tablet with me from now on. I have a new app so a client can sign right on the screen, and we'll at least have that much. I don't have to ask for money up front, but I'll have proof that the transaction took place. I might even take pictures."

He hugged Peggy and Hunter before he loaded a few quince bushes into The Potting Shed pickup and left.

"We need better evidence if we want to clear Paul's name," Hunter told her. "There has to be proof of all this."

Walter was actually upset when Peggy told him it might be better if he didn't join everyone for breakfast.

"Why? You always invite me. I was only doing what you would in this case."

"Except that I wouldn't have called the police, Walter." Peggy stopped him at the door. "You were just grandstanding for them. You knew how terrible this situation has been for me. Go home."

"I'm sorry. I thought I was doing the right thing." Walter hung his head and finally went back to his house.

Peggy and Hunter went inside to go over everything that had happened. Hunter ate what was left of the pancakes Ranson had made, and Peggy had another cup of tea.

Al looked at his notebook, as he did in every case he worked. It gave Peggy a brighter feeling for the outcome knowing he was taking it as seriously as he did his other work.

"I think the first thing we need to do is head over to Stewart's Furs. Maybe we have a chance of finding a video of this woman purchasing the coat. If someone at the store remembers her, we could put a face to a name."

"I want to be there," Paul said.

"I don't think that's a good idea," Al disagreed.

"I don't care," Paul argued. "You can't shut me out of this."

Millie put her hand on his arm. "You're already under suspicion for this murder. It's likely that the police are still asking questions at the furrier. It's not a good idea for you to be there."

Paul glared at her but didn't say anything.

"I feel the same way about you, Al," Steve said. "I know you're on vacation, but there are other things you and Paul can do without being high profile."

"Okay." Al's voice was impatient. "But I took this time off to help. I'm not sitting on my hands." He glanced at Paul who nodded back to him.

"We have the drawings Selena made," Steve reminded them. "Maybe you could use them to canvas the neighborhood where Sam sold the plants, in Brevard Court, and at the condo building where Nita Honohan was killed. We might get a hit."

Al shrugged. "Not a bad idea. We can do that, right, Paul?"

"Yeah. Sure."

Peggy hugged her son. "Just be careful, both of you. Mary Hood, or whoever she is, is dangerous. She killed that poor girl, and she's gone through a lot of trouble to set this up. We don't want to lose anyone else."

"And Peggy," Steve added. "You need to stay here and come up with that list of suspects. Just figuring out who might have it in for you and Paul could narrow the search and save a lot of time."

She felt like arguing too, but realized that what Steve said made sense. "Okay. I'll come up with a list."

Steve hugged her. "And don't take any mink coats from anyone."

"Is there somewhere online where a person could order a giant hogweed plant?" Ranson asked.

"No. The plant is being eradicated everywhere they find it. It's still creeping our way, but right now, you'd have to find some in another state and bring it here."

"It might be a good idea if we knew how the killer made the hogweed poison," Millie added.

"I know," Peggy said. "You'd like me to add that to my to-do list."

"I think that's it for now until we can get more information to go on," Steve said. "That should keep you off the street too."

"Paul, is there anything else you can add to help identify Mary Hood?" Al asked. "We could also take that drawing to Providence Cafe where you met her. Maybe someone there would recognize her. Who knows—she might be a regular."

"I can't think of anything that stood out. Unlike Sam, who was just doing something he'd done a thousand times, this was my first case as a private detective. I was nervous and wanted to get it right."

"I assume you didn't take out a yellow page ad," Peggy said. "How did she find you?"

"There is an online bulletin board that's free for private detectives to post," Paul explained. "I posted there when I first got my license about a month ago. She was the first one to call me."

"Do you still have that number?" Millie asked excitedly.

"I do—but I gave it to the police. They said it's a burner phone. No trace."

"What about contacting the bulletin board?" Peggy wondered. "Do they keep track of these things?"

"No, Mom. It's just a chat room kind of thing where you can contact a real private investigator and ask questions or set up to meet them about a job."

"Dead end, in other words." Al closed his notebook. "We'll have copies made of the drawings and then hit the streets. Call if you need anything."

Steve shook his hand. "We will. Be careful."

"You too. Come on, Paul."

"I'm coming." Paul nodded to the circle around the kitchen table. "Thanks for all your help."

Hunter had finally finished eating—she looked like a runway model—but ate like a Viking. She wiped her mouth on a napkin and handed out her card to everyone. "And if you need any legal advice or get arrested, call me."

"Thanks, Hunter." Al looked at the blue card and stuck it in his pocket.

Paul and Al left. Hunter was right behind them. That left Peggy there with her father, Norris, Millie, and Steve.

"I don't want to be a buzzkill, but you know it's not legal for us to investigate this." Norris lodged his protest with Steve.

Peggy was wondering how long it was going to take him to be annoying. She hoped he didn't plan on staying at the house after Steve and Millie were gone. She really didn't want him around.

"I think this is an unusual circumstance," Millie said. "It affects the local FBI director and his family. I'm not too sure we couldn't make a case to bring in the whole weight of the agency on this."

"Maybe," Norris half agreed. "But that's not what you're doing. You're sneaking around." He looked at Steve. "This isn't good for your reputation, sir."

"I'll worry about that later," Steve said. "There's plenty of paperwork at the office for you to catch up on. We shouldn't be long."

"That's okay," Norris said. "I'd prefer to be at your side, sir."

Peggy sighed with relief. At lease he wasn't going to be with *her*.

Steve's phone rang. It was his superior at the FBI saying that he needed to see him right away.

"I'll be back in an hour or so," he said when he was off the phone. "Millie and Norris—they want you too. Sorry, Peggy. When we're done, we'll head over to the fur shop. You're working on the lists, right?"

"Yep. You know me." She smiled. "I'll be here. Working on the lists."

Yellow Rose
The yellow rose has been prized for its cheerful hues and natural feeling of optimism. The color was difficult to find, finally located growing wild in the Middle East during the 18th century. It had one flaw – no scent for which roses were known. A beloved, sweet scent was bred into the flower, and all was well with the world!

Chapter Fifteen

Peggy only waited for Steve's SUV to leave the yard before she went upstairs to change clothes. Shakespeare watched her from the bed.

"What?" she asked the dog. "I'm not going to sit here all day making lists that I could make in five minutes. I thought from the beginning that the best person to go to Stewart's was me. If Steve and Millie go in there, looking all FBI, they aren't going to say anything to them. But if I go in, that will be a different story."

He whined and shook his head, his untrimmed ears flapping.

"Don't you start. This will go very smoothly. You'll see."

Peggy wore one of her few good outfits—a pristine white suit from Liz Claiborne. She'd had it for years, but it was timeless. She didn't like to wear it often because it picked up dirt like black picked up lint. But it was made for this occasion.

She looked at herself in the mirror, remembering where she'd worn the suit last—she'd married Steve in it. She'd felt like it was okay to wear white even though she'd been married before, just not a big, gauzy white dress with sparkles and a train.

She'd been happy with it, and her wedding flowers, specifically chosen for their meanings. She'd skipped baby's breath with its message of innocence and went for hydrangea for understanding, lily of the valley for happiness, and stephanotis for marital bliss.

Peggy enjoyed using the old Victorian language of flowers. It was exciting knowing what the blooms meant when so many other people had no idea. She could look through a floral shop and immediately choose what flowers would be right for an occasion. It was like a secret society for plant lovers.

Carefully, she put on lipstick and added blush to her cheeks. She clipped back her shoulder-length hair. She'd never dyed her hair with its white-tinged red, despite being married to a man ten years younger. She'd lived through every bit of that white and those wrinkles on her face. She was proud of each one.

When she was done, she slipped her feet into Jimmy Choo sandals that she'd also worn for her wedding and was ready to go.

It was an unfortunate coincidence that her mother had a migraine and had kicked her father out of their bedroom. He'd been about to knock on Peggy's door as she opened it.

His eyes got wide as he looked at her. "You are something beautiful this morning, baby girl. I was wondering what I was going to do with myself until your mother feels better. Now I know."

"Dad—"

"Don't even start trying to tell me that you aren't going

to Stewart's Furs." He held up his hand as if to ward off her excuse. "That's exactly where you're headed since Steve couldn't go. I'll go with you."

"It won't be good for you to go," Peggy protested as she walked quickly past him to the stairs. "I have to do this alone. It's better for the subterfuge."

"Nonsense. I could be your sugar daddy, looking to buy you a new fur coat. It would work. I think your mother threw a sport coat into that pile of clothes she brought. I'll only be a minute."

"Dad—"

"It will be much better with two of us there. You know it will." He grinned at her, his eyes alight with cunning humor. "Two heads are always better than one. Besides, if you don't let me go, I'll call Steve. I have him on speed dial, you know. Paul set that up for me. It's very fast. I only push one button, and there he is."

Peggy sighed. She wasn't going to win this argument. "All right. But hurry. Maybe this will work out—you can make out my list of suspects as I drive."

"You can't drive. Your car doesn't look like it belongs to a cute babe and her sugar daddy. We'll take my car. *You* can make out the list."

But this was an argument Peggy had the upper hand in. "You're right. My hybrid doesn't scream money. But neither does your Volvo. However, Paul just had the Rolls cleaned and tuned. We'll take it."

No way Ranson could argue with that.

The 1940 Silver Shadow was a classic. It had been part of the estate. John had never driven it, not liking the status it conveyed. For a few years Peggy had toyed with the engine, trying to convert it to hydrogen, but she'd given up before the task was finished.

Paul had surprised her and had the original engine restored and the rest of the car cleaned so it could be driven. He'd borrowed it once or twice to impress Mai and

her family. Otherwise the Rolls-Royce slept covered in a
tarp in the garage.

Peggy removed the soft tarp and folded it neatly before
putting it in the trunk.

Ranson ran his hand appreciatively across the car's
shiny finish. "You're right. Nothing tops this. I'd forgotten
how beautiful it is."

"Let's get in. Steve's meeting might not last very long.
I want to be in and out of Stewart's before he knows we're
there."

"Okay, Honey Bunny."

"Don't call me that, and don't pretend to be my sugar
daddy. Can't you just be my wealthy father buying me a
mink for my birthday?"

"I can do that, but it won't be as much fun," he
grumbled.

Stewart's Furs was a hole in the wall shop in Myer's
Park. It was hard to tell that so many expensive furs were
sold here every year. It was a very popular place for local
bankers—and their wives and mistresses.

Peggy was opposed to wearing fur and had never
owned a fur coat in her life. But she parked the Rolls
outside the shop and pretended like she belonged there.
Ranson came around and opened the door for her. She
thanked him regally, and they proceeded into the place
together.

The shop was shabby, which probably added to its
popularity. Stewart Purl saw their entrance and the car. He
immediately pushed aside his only sales clerk to wait on
them himself.

He was a small man, barely five feet, with tiny hands
and feet. He was dressed in a perfect gray suit and white
shirt. His white hair and mustache were well-groomed.

Smiling, he presented himself to Peggy and Ranson.

"Good morning. May I help you?"

Ranson nodded. "Yes, my good man. I would like to buy a beautiful new coat for my beautiful daughter."

Peggy sighed with relief. She hadn't thought he could pull off the sugar daddy routine convincingly, and he was her father—*eww*.

Stewart kissed her hand. "You are a lovely young woman. I'm sure we can find something equally as beautiful for you to wear."

"Equally?" Ranson thundered. "Are you saying you have a coat as beautiful as my daughter?"

Stewart backed down from his statement. "No. Of course not. I meant a coat that will show off your beautiful daughter. Of course there is nothing more beautiful than she."

Peggy narrowed her eyes at her father, giving him an unspoken request to get on with it. "I'm looking for the same coat that a friend of mine purchased here. It was full-length brown mink."

"Oh yes? We have many of those. If you will step this way, madam."

Peggy started to follow him and then hung back. "I want *exactly* the same coat, you understand."

He paused. "Surely. We have many such requests. What is your friend's name?"

"Her name is Mary Hood. Do you know the coat I mean?"

"I don't recall the name, but I can check my files." He snapped his fingers.

His sales clerk, a plain little woman with her brown hair rolled up in a bun on the back of her head, was standing close by. She wore large, black-rimmed glasses that did nothing to make her face attractive, and a shapeless dress. Even her nametag was blank, as though Mr. Purl didn't want her to be noticed at all.

"I can take the name of your friend and look her up,"

she told Peggy.

"Mary Hood. She and I have been friends forever," Peggy gushed, wondering if she had overplayed herself when the woman looked at her like she had a loose screw.

"I'll check on that, ma'am."

Stewart, Ranson, and Peggy waited for her to return, making small talk.

The inside of the shop was in no better condition that the outside. The upholstery on the green chairs near the dressing room was threadbare. The carpet needed to be replaced. Even the dark green drapes had seen better days. She wondered why Stewart didn't reinvest in the shop. Maybe he was near retirement and just wanted to get by.

The dowdy sales clerk returned promptly and whispered in Stewart's ear.

He smiled at Peggy. "I'm afraid no one by that name has purchased a coat with us, at least not recently. Could she have used another name? Sometimes ladies who visit us are reluctant to use their real names."

Peggy exchanged glances with Ranson.

"What about another friend—Nita Honohan?" Peggy asked.

The sales clerk scurried away to check the records. She returned with the same expression on her overworked face. Nita Honohan wasn't listed in the records either.

"I don't understand," Peggy said. "Maybe I have the wrong shop. I thought for sure she said Stewart's."

"And I'm certain she did." The proprietor smiled uneasily, no doubt feeling the lucrative sale slipping through his fingers. "Perhaps she used a different name."

"I can't think what other name she might have used." Peggy tapped her finger on her bag. "She's such a trickster though, anything is possible. Could I have a peek at the sales book in case I might recognize her name?"

It was clear Mr. Purl wasn't happy with that idea. "I don't think that would be a good business practice, do you? I'm sure you wouldn't want someone to see your name in here if you were trying to keep something secret."

"You're right." Peggy sighed and stared at the floor.

"Perhaps if we knew what the lady in question looked like," the assistant added. "Can you describe her?"

Peggy hadn't actually seen her and was at a loss to describe the woman who had appeared so different in the sketches from Sam and Paul.

Ranson took her hand. "Don't worry, honey. I'm sure we can find something you like at another shop. I could get that new coat for your mama and your sister at the same time."

It was a brilliant move. Knowing he would lose all three sales, Stewart immediately led them to a small back room where fur coats were being altered and cleaned. When they were seated at a card table, he had his sales clerk bring out the book.

"I hope I don't have to ask for your discretion. People trust me to keep their secrets." He smiled slyly at Ranson. "I understand that a lovely younger woman isn't always a man's *daughter*—if you know what I mean."

Peggy had to put her hand to her mouth to keep from laughing. It seemed that the truth wasn't always what people wanted to hear.

A discreet chime at the front door announced a new customer. Stewart excused himself and went to wait on his new customers.

When he was gone, Ranson snickered. "See? Even though I'm really your father, he wanted me to be your sugar daddy."

Peggy ignored him and looked through the sales book for recent sales of a full-length brown mink. Luckily the store was small, and Mr. Purl didn't have to sell many coats to make a living.

She was about to point out a sale in the last month when she heard Steve's voice outside in the main shop area.

"Holy smokes! It's the Feds!" Ranson whispered.

Green Moss
Moss is believed to have evolved from algae. The plants do not have vascular tissue which other plants use to transport water and nutrients. Mosses don't have roots, stems, or flowers for this reason.

Chapter Sixteen

"It's Steve and Millie." Peggy peeked through the green curtain that obscured the back room from the sales floor. "That was a quick meeting."

"But you were right. They're showing their badges. Nothing undercover for them."

"We have to get out of here. But we need the names and address of those buyers. None of them jump off the page at me, but some leg work might give us better answers."

"I can write pretty quickly," her father volunteered.

"We don't need that." Peggy took out her cell phone. "We can just take pictures of the information. Check around for a back door out of here."

She took pictures of the five people who'd purchased the brown mink coats. This gave her their addresses and phone numbers as well as their names. She realized these might not be their real names—Stewart didn't seem all that surprised by her request. Still, there might be some truth in the numbers, especially if the buyers bought with credit cards.

"I found another door," Ranson said. "Are you really that upset about Steve finding you here?"

"Not exactly. But I did say I'd stay home and work on that list. He worries so much. I hate to make it worse for him, bless his heart."

Ranson chuckled. "Then we'd better get out of here. The Rolls might be a dead giveaway."

"I don't think so. He knows I never take it out."

Stewart was showing his FBI visitors to the already occupied back room. Peggy and her father slipped out into the alley through the back door. They hurried out to the Rolls and got away cleanly.

Ranson hooted and slapped his leg as they started up Selwyn Avenue where the fur shop was located. "It's always a rush. I love working with you, Margaret."

"You'd better not tell Mom. You know she feels like everything is bad for your heart."

"Don't remind me. She's forbidden me pizza. Can you believe it? Pizza! One of my favorite foods. I have to sneak out and get it."

"Or eat it at my house."

"I know she means well, but life is about having a good time between bouts of working. If you're not having a good time, what's the point?"

Peggy smiled. "I agree, but I also love you, Dad. I don't want you to have another heart attack."

"I don't either, although the last one wasn't so bad."

He grinned at her, and she laughed.

"I saw the scar where they cut you open. It was bad."

Peggy pulled the Rolls into the driveway at her house. Ranson helped her cover the car in the garage again. They'd closed the garage door just a moment before Steve and Millie got there.

"Remember," Ranson whispered. "Mum's the word. I won't talk even if they water- board me."

"Steve isn't going to waterboard anyone. The FBI doesn't do things like that."

"Yeah, right. The FBI is in cahoots with the CIA. When they don't torture people, it's because they hand them over to the CIA to do it. I've watched those YouTube videos. Being American doesn't protect you anymore."

"Okay. Hush now." Peggy smiled as she greeted her husband. "Steve! That was a short meeting."

"I guess that was a problem for you since you didn't stick around at the fur shop to say hello."

"What are you talking about?" Ranson asked. "We've been right here all morning, writing down the names of people who want to kill Peggy. It's a long list."

Steve crouched and stared at the driveway. "There is always a little dirt and moss from the garage when the Rolls goes out. No one bothered to put a real floor in there. And how many people in Charlotte drive a vintage Rolls like that one?"

"Probably quite a few," Peggy said. "But I'm not going to lie to you. We came up with a plan and went for it. We got some names and other personal info that might belong to the killer."

"You said you were staying here," Steve reminded her. "You could be a target for this person. I'm sure you know that."

"Let's go inside to argue." Peggy took his arm. "I see Walter peeking out at us with his binoculars. He knows how to read lips. He probably knows what we just said and is picking up his phone to call the police."

But she was mistaken. Walter came slowly out of his house and walked through the paths he'd created in the flower beds to join them.

"Steve. Peggy. I just wanted to apologize for my

actions this morning. I guess I got carried away with my duties as the forensic botanist for the city. It won't happen again. I hope you can forgive me."

Peggy knew Walter was eccentric and overzealous but still a friend.

"It's okay. Just remember when all this is over, we'll still be neighbors. I don't want your work or mine to jeopardize our relationship, do you?"

"No. Of course not." He shook hands with Steve and Ranson. "Is there anything I can do to help?"

She smiled and took his arm. "We're going to have coffee and tea. Would you like to join us?"

"Very much so. Thank you." He patted her hand. "I'm afraid I have some bad news from the investigation front. I thought you should know. The police are coming to your house sometime today to search your basement lab for signs of giant hogweed."

"What? Did you tell them there is no hogweed growing in my basement?" she asked him. "You were just there a few days ago."

"I know. And I tried to tell them. They wouldn't listen. Captain Hager feels like the link between you being an expert on botanical poisons and Paul killing the woman on Providence Road is going to solve the case for him. He won't hear any other theories about it."

"Thanks for the warning." Peggy bit her lip, thinking about all the damage that could be done to her experiments. "At least if I'm here, I can supervise."

"Idiots." Ranson stalked toward the house. "Why am I paying their salaries?"

Walter waited outside for the police to arrive, not wanting them to think that he wasn't on their side even though he had warned Peggy of their arrival.

Steve and Millie were interested in the information

Peggy got at the fur store. Steve had showed Stewart Purl and his sales clerk the drawings Selena had done.

"This one with the shorter hair looked familiar to them," he said. "But they have no video surveillance, and they couldn't put the face to a name. She's not one of their regulars."

Peggy squinted at the drawing of the short-haired woman. There was something vaguely familiar about her. She couldn't put her finger on it, but she reminded her of someone.

"Remembering something?" Steve asked.

"Maybe. But I can't tell for sure." She took out her phone. "I'll send you the names of the people who bought brown mink coats. They each purchased recently and only got the one coat. Maybe it's something."

Shakespeare jumped up and ran to the door, barking. His warning was followed by a knock at the kitchen door.

As Peggy expected, it was an all too eager Captain Hager, holding out his search warrant for her basement.

"Are you ready for your close up, Dr. Lee?"

Walter winked at Peggy as he came inside with the officers. He followed them down the basement stairs as though he'd only just arrived.

Knowing the police were coming to search her basement and actually going through it were two different things for Peggy. She switched on all the lights so they could clearly see the plants. She had nothing to hide, and everything to lose if they made a mess here.

"Please be careful with my experiments," she pleaded. "There are no poisonous plants here, Captain, but some of these projects are delicate and have been ongoing for years."

Captain Hager hailed Walter. "Can you tell if there are any poisons here?"

"As I told you this morning, there are no poisons down here. I've spent time here recently, and Peggy doesn't grow botanical poisons. She does grow new species that can be used to feed hungry children around the world. Bear that in mind."

"Peggy, huh?" Captain Hager snorted. "Maybe we should find a local botanist who doesn't know Dr. Lee so well."

Walter laughed. "Good luck with that. Dr. Lee is well known locally as well as internationally. Her reputation speaks for itself. She is always above reproach."

"Yeah. So does that poison gunk her son put in the victim's coat. Out of the way if you aren't going to help, Dr. Bellows."

"Captain!" One of the young officers called to him. "Isn't the giant hogweed supposed to be tall? Look at these plants over here."

Captain Hager gave Peggy and Walter a grin as though he'd found her secret stash. "I'm coming, Bartlett. Whatever you do, don't touch the stuff."

All the officers gathered around the tall spinach plants. Captain Hager stared at the plants like he was waiting for a sign to pop up saying they were hogweed.

"The ME says not to cut this stuff because the juice is deadly," he said. "Bartlett, put on those big gloves they gave us and get a sample."

Peggy ran to put herself between the spinach and the officers. "No need for that. This is a new breed of spinach. It's not poisonous."

"Says you," Hager retorted. "Step aside, Dr. Lee, and let us do our job."

She ripped off one of the leaves and rubbed it on her bare hands and arms before eating it. The officers, even Captain Hager, took a step back and held their breath.

Spinach
Spinach is believed to have originated in ancient Persia and then spread to India and China. There are records of it being eaten as far back as 827 AD. When Catherine de Medici of Florence became queen of France she loved spinach so much that she insisted it be served at every meal.

Chapter Seventeen

A moment later, Walter did the same. Steve and Millie smiled from the staircase.

"Now what, sir?" Bartlett asked. "They should be burned and dying now, right? That's what the information packet said."

"We're not burned or dying," Peggy challenged them. "I told you, this is broad-leaf spinach. It's going to feed thousands of hungry people around the world in a shorter growing time. Would you like a taste? It's delicious."

Captain Hager had a disgusted look on his face as he ordered his officers away from the spinach. "You think this is funny, don't you? You know more than the stupid police officers. That's quite an accomplishment, except that you only know a lot about plants."

"I was married to a police detective for more than thirty years. Some of my best friends are still on the job. I never think the police are stupid, but you're not experts in every field, including botany."

He ignored her and walked away, searching through the myriad plants across the basement. Because they had a better idea of what they were looking for this time, the search went quickly. Once the spinach was ascertained to be harmless, there was nothing else that came close to the description of hogweed.

Thirty minutes later, the officers were headed outside to their cars. Captain Hager looked surprised to see Al and Paul upstairs in the kitchen.

"I see we're all as thick as thieves around here," he remarked. "You better watch yourselves on this, ladies and gentlemen. There is a lot more than one officer's career on the chopping block. Have a nice day."

When they were gone, Peggy sank down on one of the kitchen chairs as Steve and Millie related the details of the search.

Despite Captain Hager's assertion that this was pleasant for her, she was used to being on the other side of the investigation. Her curiosity had led her to become a contract botanist for the police department. She enjoyed her sometimes challenging work with them as they looked for criminals.

She didn't like people looking at her or Paul on the other side of that thin line.

"Are you okay, Peggy?" Al asked as everyone discussed what they'd discovered that morning.

"I'm fine." She smiled at him. "Just ready for this to be over. I guess I'd make a nervous bad guy."

"It's gonna be fine. We got a couple of hits on the drawings we showed around. I think the woman with the short hair is our suspect. She must've only used the long hair wig trick with Sam. "She's smart, but we're smarter. You'll see."

"Where is everyone?" Peggy heard her mother call

from the marble stairway. "What's going on?"

Ranson went to get her.

"So it looks like we have a few things to move forward with," Steve said.

"Oh Margaret!" Her mother's voice called out from the main hall. "Have you seen this poor tree today? What's wrong with it?"

The tone was much different in her father's voice as he called for her to come quickly. "Margaret! I think your spruce is dying."

Peggy was the first one in the main hall with her parents. Everyone else followed. She looked up at the blue spruce she'd planted when she was first married.

It was easy to see why her parents were concerned. The top of the tree was bending over, and the branches were curled and dying. Many of them had already turned brown.

"Have you been watering the poor thing?" Lilla asked.

"Of course she's been watering it." Ranson deflected his wife's acidic tone. "This is something else."

Peggy examined the tree carefully. Of course it was going to die someday—no plant, tree, or person lived forever. But this wasn't a normal death.

The tree had been healthy last month when she'd done her semi-annual checkup on it. It should have had years to live.

"Help me with the floor, Paul," Peggy said.

She and John had a special trap door put in the wood floor so they could get to the roots of the tree that were growing from a deep, ceramic well that had been created for it. The base of the tree reached up from the basement area through the hole in the floor.

"Should we go down into the basement to look at it?" Paul asked.

"No." Peggy had seen what she needed. When the trap door had been opened, a plastic vial with dozens of holes in it dropped to the floor at her feet. She used a pair of gloves that she'd always kept in the antique table at the foot of the circular stairs to protect her hands when she worked on the prickly boughs.

"Someone poisoned it." She held the vial up to her nose and sniffed it. "Someone came into the house and killed my tree."

There was a painful sob stuck in her throat that she refused to release. She pushed past her friends and hurried to the basement where she could analyze the poison.

Steve followed quickly behind her. "Wait, Peggy. Maybe you shouldn't try to do that yourself."

"Why not?" she demanded. "Someone came into our house and did this—probably this morning when I went outside to help Sam with the plan shipment. I forgot to set the alarm or lock the door. I want to know what's in this and who did it."

"Is there something I can do to help?"

Her green eyes were calm and cold. "Go back upstairs. Look for the killer. Don't let anyone else come down here."

He started to speak again but gave up, nodded, and went upstairs.

Hundreds of memories rushed through Peggy's mind. All the Christmas celebrations with Paul and John held at the base of the growing spruce. Years of tending the tree and watching it grow. The day she'd told John about her idea to plant a tree in the old house. The tiny spruce that had stood tall in the main hall. It had been barely a sapling that they passed each day.

She refused to cry as she dumped the rest of the poison into a pot and began experimenting on it. Various chemical compounds responded to her tests. Whoever had poisoned the spruce knew exactly what they were doing—as they had with the hogweed in the lining of the mink coat.

When she'd finished her testing, she sat in the office chair she kept at her desk in the basement. It was too late to save the spruce. Enough of the poison in the cylinder had gone into the dirt and roots to keep her from stopping it.

Shakespeare had stayed in the basement with her. He whined as he stared at her, as though he felt the terrible sorrow that was clutching at her heart.

"There's nothing we can do," she whispered to him. "It's dead. We might as well have someone remove it."

He rolled over and covered his eyes with his paws.

"Who could hate me enough—and know me so well—to do something like this? It has to be connected to the garden shop and setting Paul up for the murder. I understand that, but I can't imagine who I've harmed so badly that they would want this revenge on me."

Peggy sat there for a while longer, taking it all in and wondering what the next thing would be. This was obviously a personal campaign to hurt and embarrass her, maybe ruin her entire life.

She had to find a way to stop this. She had to figure out who was behind it.

Blue Spruce

Blue spruce is rarely used for lumber because the wood is brittle and full of knots. But because of its lovely shape and color, along with its thick boughs, it is planted in landscape settings.

Chapter Eighteen

Peggy finally went upstairs. Ranson and Lilla had remained behind. Al and Paul had gone back out to find more information about the woman in the drawing. Millie had gone to join Norris at the office. Steve was nursing a glass of whiskey at the kitchen table.

When they saw her, Walter was first on his feet.

"Let me take a look at it. My specialty is trees, remember? I can probably save it."

"It's too late." Peggy told him the chemicals and their amounts that she'd found in the poison vial. "There is no way to save it. We both know it."

Walter hung his head. "I'm so sorry, my dear. Do you think one of the police officers did this today?"

"I don't think so. It's been a few hours." She put the kettle on to boil. "I think it happened this morning, but it may have been formulated to be fast-acting."

"You have an alarm," Lilla said. "No one can go in and out without you knowing. How could this happen?"

"The same thing happened with The Potting Shed alarm," Steve added. "What company is the house alarm with, Peggy?"

"I had Dalton change alarm companies to the same one Brevard Court uses for the shops." Peggy felt a flutter in her chest as she said it. "Does that mean whoever is doing this works at the alarm company?"

"It's possible." Steve put his arm around her. "I've heard of cases like this before. I'm going to talk to someone at the company, and we'll see what's going on. Please stay here with your parents."

Peggy wrote the name of the company on a slip of paper. "Why? Whoever did this could have poisoned me at the same time but didn't."

"Please." Steve's brown eyes stared into hers. "Let's not take any chances."

The kettle whistled. She nodded. "All right."

Peggy stayed at the house with her parents. She spent the time on her computer looking up the names of the people she'd taken from the fur shop. If there was anything suspicious about them at all, she couldn't find it. She also came up with a list of people who might hate her. The names were from cases she'd helped the police solve.

She figured out the approximate amounts of hogweed to the other poison plants in the mixture that had killed Nita Honohan and texted it to Millie.

At that point, her mind just wouldn't let her go any farther. She sat, staring at her computer, until a chime sounded on her phone letting her know that she had a call.

It was her friend, Nightflyer.

"I'm so sorry," he said. "I've been out of town."

"There was nothing you could do."

"Do you know who's done these things?"

"No. The police are still trying to figure it out. They

don't have much to go on."

"But you have a feeling?"

"I have no idea who could hate me this much."

"You're letting your emotions cloud your analytical skills."

"Maybe."

"You have to be sharp about this. I'll do what I can to help from here."

"Where's here?"

"Hong Kong. And I only tell you that because I'm leaving."

"I'm sorry. Is there nowhere you can hide?"

"No. And there is nowhere the woman stalking you can hide either. Not if you really look for her."

"Do you know who she is?"

"No. I wish I did. Be careful. From the pattern of her actions, she wants you to be terrified before she kills you. Don't give her that luxury."

"Thanks."

But there was no reply.

Peggy had no idea who Nightflyer really was. She'd started playing online chess with him after John's death. He'd told her they could never meet. Now she suspected he might know who actually killed John, and why.

He'd been on the run the last few years after trying to get away from his past life. He never stayed anywhere for more than a day or two. She thought he might be a spy or some government official.

She wished he would have had a better explanation for what had been happening to her. A lot of times he knew things before the police even though he was thousands of miles away. She pictured him in a room with dozens of computers and newsfeed coming in from all over the world keeping him updated.

And yet it seemed he couldn't even save himself. How did she expect him to know how to save her?

For a while, before they were married, Peggy had
suspected Steve of being Nightflyer. There was that night
in the park across the street where she was supposed to
meet her computer friend. Steve had been there, supposedly
keeping an eye on her.

Once they were married, Steve had such hard feelings
about Nightflyer that she couldn't imagine it was him
anymore.

"Get your head together, Peggy." She looked at the
people on the furrier's list and the people on her list of
possible suspects.

What did they have in common?

What was the one important clue she couldn't tell from
their names and addresses?

"I can't tell what you look like." She circled the names
of the three women on Stewart Purl's list. The killer was
careful with her identity. She went to great lengths to
disguise herself from Paul and Sam. She could be anyone.

She looked at the list of people she'd sent to jail. She'd
barely known most of them—some of them not at all.

"It can't be one of those people. They'd only be
guessing at what they could do to get back at me. This has
to be someone who knows me personally."

Peggy circled the only name on the list that matched
all the criteria—Ruth Sargent.

Years ago a good friend of hers, a specialist in
underwater forensics, had an affair and killed the man who
loved her. The police had asked Peggy to look at a plant
that was twined in the victim's hair. She'd identified it as
duckweed. Then she'd met her old friend, Ruth, who was
working on the double homicide, also working for the
police.

Peggy hadn't put the facts together until after
everything was over. She'd realized that Ruth had killed

her lover and his wife. Once she knew that Ruth had committed the perfect murders, and made a fool of her in the process, Peggy felt that she had to call the police.

Ruth had been arrested and been charged with the murders. She was serving two life sentences somewhere in the state. She couldn't be out of prison yet.

Peggy called Al. She asked him about the case that had involved her old college friend.

"Sure. I remember that. There's no way she's part of this. I can understand why you'd think she could be. But she's still in prison."

"Are you sure? Is there any way to check?"

"I can check with a phone call, Peggy. But there's no way she's out yet, not even for good behavior. I'll call the prison and let you know for sure."

"Thanks, Al."

Peggy put her phone in her pocket and turned her mind to how it was possible to make the paste she'd found in the lining of Nita Honohan's mink coat.

Of course any plant, poisonous or not, could be made into salves and ointments. It was where the first medicines came from. All someone needed were the basic elements of the plant—flowers, leaves, berries, roots, or stems. Any of those could be, and had been, made into gels, powders, and other topical solutions.

But if she was correct, and her stalker was Ruth, where did she get the idea? Ruth was clever, but she wasn't a botanist. Putting together a poison solution to kill the tree she knew Peggy loved was one thing. Figuring out what to do with the giant hogweed was another.

Still, it was possible. Ruth was intelligent and resourceful, as she'd found to her chagrin.

Peggy looked through her journals that arrived monthly from various botanical groups and institutions. There were several mentions of hogweed and its march through the U.S. Everyone was worried about what would happen when it came into contact with larger numbers of people.

She couldn't find anything about experiments being done with hogweed. She checked everywhere she could think of online, but there was nothing.

Her father brought her a cup of orange spice tea, one of her favorites.

"How's it going?" he asked.

"I think it's possible that I know who's behind all of this. Ruth Sargent. She specializes in underwater forensics. I don't know how much of a leap that would be into botany, but it makes sense."

Peggy explained about their friendship and turning Ruth over to the police. "Al says she's still in prison, but he's checking to make sure. Right now, she's the only one that was my friend for many years, and would know all about me. I think she'd be capable of doing this."

"But if she's in prison, Margaret, that wouldn't make any sense."

"I know." She sipped her tea. "We'll see what Al has to say."

Her phone rang. It was Al.

"Well, I found Ruth Sargent," he said. "She's not in prison."

Peggy's heart fluttered as she carefully set down her cup of tea.

"She escaped? Shouldn't we have known about that?"

"You could say she escaped. Actually, she died last year."

Arrowhead
Also known as Indian Potato because their tuberous roots can be eaten like potatoes. Native American women collected the plants by digging them out of the water with their toes. They were baked in fires and were a staple of their diet. Mostly wild today but also used as pond plants for indoor gardens.

Chapter Nineteen

"Are you sure?" Peggy asked.

"Yeah. Pretty sure. She was killed in a knife fight at the prison. There was an autopsy and everything. She's not our killer."

Ranson waited until Peggy said goodbye to Al.

"So not the person you thought," he guessed.

"No." Peggy thought hard about Ruth. "She was the only one I could think of. How could anyone else know where I lived, what I did, and exactly where to hurt me?"

He hugged her. "You'll come up with another name. There's someone out there you're not thinking about, honey. Maybe you should get off the computer for a while and come downstairs with your mother and me."

"You know, Dad. I think I'll get away from the computer for a while, but I'm heading to The Potting Shed."

"There's nothing you can do there right now. And you promised Steve you'd stay here so we know you're safe."

"Dad, I—"

Her phone rang again. This time it was Bobby Dean.

"Peggy, I just wanted to give you a status update on your claim for The Potting Shed. The police have finished their investigation into the break-in and vandalism. They have no suspects at this time but have assured me that they will continue to look into it."

"Does that leave you clear to write me a check for the damages?"

"There's only one thing that still bites my butt. What happened to the alarm company? I haven't been able to get any answers out of them. I've never had this problem before. I'm reluctant to release those funds until we know that your shop will be adequately protected."

"I understand. I'm reluctant to put new things in there, too, until a new alarm system is set up."

"If it wouldn't be too much trouble, I was wondering if you could meet me at the shop today. The techs from the alarm company are supposed to be there surveying the damage and giving us an idea of what happened."

Peggy smiled at her father. "I'd be happy to meet you there, Bobby. What time?"

"I'm headed that way now. Let's say thirty minutes?"

"That's fine. It would be nice to get all of this out of the way."

"Thank you, Peggy. I'll see you then."

"I suppose you're proud of yourself," Ranson said after she was finished on the phone. "You found a way out. But you're not going alone. I'll call Sam, Paul, and Al to meet us there. Maybe I'll call Steve and Hunter too."

"That's fine, Dad. I think they'll be a little bored talking to my insurance adjuster, but call them all. Maybe Mom would like to go too."

"I could shake you sometimes." He shook his head

instead. "You're as stubborn as your mother."

"Stubborn? What about you?"

"I'm stubborn, but I have other redeeming qualities that offset it."

"Wait until I tell Mom that. I'm sure we'd both like to hear about your *redeeming qualities*."

"Well, no matter what, you're not leaving this house alone. Just get used to it."

Peggy sighed and went downstairs with her father and Shakespeare at her heels.

Lilla didn't feel her presence would make much difference if someone wanted to kill her daughter. "I'll stay here and keep an eye on things."

"And what are you going to do if the killer shows up at the door?" Peggy asked.

Lilla pulled a small, pearl-handle revolver out of her handbag. "I've been shooting since I was a little girl. I'm not worried about killing someone who might be after my family. You two go on. I'll hold down the fort here."

Ranson and Peggy left, meeting Walter as they walked out of the house.

"I'm glad to see you," he told Peggy. "I've been looking around all morning for any research where hogweed may have been used as a poison in a homicide before. No one has ever heard of such a thing. I'm hitting a dead end even at my conspiracy sites. Do you have any information?"

"No, she doesn't." Ranson took Peggy's arm as he started toward the car. "And if she did, she wouldn't share it with you after you stole her job."

Peggy took her arm from her father and turned back to her friend. "I've been doing the same thing all morning, Walter. I've hit several dead ends with the poison and the suspect I had in mind. I don't think I can help you right now."

Walter glanced up at Ranson's lean body that was

much taller than his. "Thank you for your help. Perhaps
you could explain to others that I haven't taken your
position with the city. It is only for this case."

Her father didn't respond. He got in the car on the
passenger side and closed the door.

Peggy got in the car too. "If I'm okay with what
happened between me and Walter, you should be too. He
didn't know what he was doing this morning. But he made
up for it by preparing me for the police raid on my
basement."

No matter what she said, he was angry at her neighbor.
Talk about being stubborn!

They reached The Potting Shed at the same time as
Bobby Dean and parked close together behind the shop. It
was sad to see Brevard Court bustling and the garden shop
closed. She had to remind herself that it wouldn't be this
way much longer.

They let themselves in through the back door. There
was no sign of the alarm company yet. Peggy left the door
open to get some air inside. She couldn't do the same with
the front door, or she'd risk turning away customers.

Everything was as they'd left it. The space looked
oddly empty and sad after years of being filled to the brim.
Peggy was excited to see the little lizard sitting on the side
of the pond sunning himself. At least that hadn't changed.

If you could only talk, she considered.

There was a knock at the front door. Two men in gray
uniforms waited impatiently for her to open it.

"We're here from the alarm company."

"Yes." She stood back and let them in.

Bobby and Peggy introduced themselves to the men.

"I have a few questions," Bobby said. "Did you bring
your supervisor with you?"

The alarm company employees glanced at each other

as though they had no idea what he was talking about.

"No. We're here to repair the alarm. No one mentioned answering questions. Our supervisor is out of town."

"I'm sorry, but I can't allow you to repair this alarm and have it connected to the service again," Bobby said. "At least not until we know why the alarm wasn't triggered at your end when it was cut."

The two techs shrugged, clearly out of their depths.

"Sorry," the first tech said. "But if we don't reconnect the alarm today, it could be a week before we'll be back."

Bobby frowned. "I'm sorry, Peggy, but I just can't authorize this."

"I guess that's that." She smiled at the men from the alarm service and handed them her business card. "Could you get someone to give me a call? I'd like to get this done, but I need the insurance company to be happy with it too."

One of the men took the card and stuffed it into his pocket. "You know all the alarms in Brevard court and Latta Arcade are with the same leasing company, and we do all their work. Eventually, you'll have to hook up with us whether you like it or not."

Peggy wasn't happy with his tone, but he wasn't the one she needed to talk to. "Just have your supervisor give me a call when he's back. Thanks."

They seemed dumbfounded at being turned away, but eventually they left, hurrying down the cobblestones toward their truck parked on the street.

"Now what?" Ranson asked. "You can't open your business again until this is settled?"

Peggy and Ranson both stared at Bobby.

He didn't back down from his original statement. "I'm sorry. I'm going to meet with someone from the security firm again. I need to know that the alarm problem isn't going to happen again. I'm sure you want that peace of mind too."

Peggy agreed that it was important. But so was getting

The Potting Shed up and running again. She couldn't restock a shelf or order more plants until this was settled.

"I understand, even though I don't like it. Thanks for your help."

"We'll get through this, Peggy." Bobby shook her hand. "Trust me. We want you back in business too."

Bobby nodded to Ranson and then left too.

Peggy waved goodbye to him and took out her phone.

"Calling Steve?" her father asked.

"Maybe he's got the answers we need from the alarm company."

But Steve didn't answer, and Peggy had to leave him a message. She was ready to leave when Emil and Sofia came through the front door.

"Oh my God!" Sofia threw her arms around Peggy. "What you've been through. No one should have to go through this. Come back with us to The Kozy Kettle. We'll make you food, and you'll feel better."

Lavender

While lavender has been used for hundreds of years, it is considered unsafe to apply to the skin of young boys. Lavender oil has a hormonal effect that could disrupt the normal hormone balance in a boy's body. Lavender also has a calming effect on the central nervous system that may be harmful during surgery. Do not use at least two weeks prior to surgery.

Chapter Twenty

Emil's thick gray mustache wiggled as he agreed with his wife. "You haven't been eating. Look at you—wasting away because that worthless husband of yours can't protect you. We have a cousin, Milo. He's not much to look at, but he's rich. You'd never have to work another day in your life."

Emil and Sofia had first met Peggy when she was alone, after John's death. They had always tried to play matchmaker with her then, and the tradition continued. The couple had never grown to like Steve. They thought he was bad for her and that she should get rid of him to marry one of their many family members.

"I'm fine." Peggy smiled. *Was there ever a time when she was less fine than this?* "I'm eating, and I'm working at home until we get the go-ahead to re-open the shop. I'm sure your cousin is very nice, but I really love Steve and want to stay married to him."

Sofia's jangly bracelets jingled as she hurriedly

crossed herself. "You don't have to pretend with us. How long have we known you? We've known you long enough to see you're unhappy."

Emil agreed. "Come over for some garlic soup anyway. It will fix you right up. We'll talk about your husband—and the man you should have."

If Emil and Sofia weren't such good friends in every other way, Peggy would have stopped associating with them long ago. But she didn't want to allow a small idiosyncrasy to ruin their friendship.

When she didn't answer right away, Emil took her hand in his big, work-worn one. "At least tell me you'll have your weekly flower club meeting tomorrow night. I'm making scones for you."

"Of course."

It was the last thing she wanted to do knowing everyone who'd be there would want to talk about Paul and The Potting Shed. But maybe something normal would be good. "I'll be there at seven. Thank you both for being such good friends.

Emil and Sofia both hugged her and Ranson extensively. They walked back across the cobblestones to their shop, whispering, and Peggy locked the front door behind them.

As she did, she glanced at the picture of her and John that she'd framed and put on the shop wall when she'd first opened. She'd been so determined to follow through on the dream they'd shared. Nothing could have stopped her.

She turned around and stared at what was left of that dream. Everything was gone, but it was more than she'd started with all those years ago. She'd brought The Potting Shed to life once before, and she'd do it again.

"You still miss him, don't you?" Ranson asked as he watched her.

"Of course. I'll always miss him. But I love Steve. They are two different men. It doesn't seem possible to love them both, but I do, Dad."

"The girl who fell in love with John is a different person than the woman who fell in love with Steve."

She smiled and hugged him. "When did you get so wise? I don't remember you being so smart when I was younger."

"You just didn't appreciate how smart I was." He chuckled. "And I'm still getting better. Just like you, sweetheart."

"Let's get home before someone misses me. Maybe there's good news waiting. And I have to call someone to take down my tree."

They rode back home together. Sam called to let her know he'd planted what he'd taken that day from the house and managed to sell another two thousand dollars' worth of the previous order.

"I've only got three thousand left to go," he said. "I think I'll be able to break even on this. Where are you?"

"Leaving The Potting Shed and heading home." She explained about the alarm system.

"Listen, Peggy, we've gotta get up and running again before people forget who we are. I'll sleep at the shop with a shotgun if I have to until the alarm is back on."

She laughed at his eagerness to reopen. He was almost as bad as her.

"I'm not sure about that idea, but we'll work something out. I'll see you in a little while."

Steve was back at the house, sharing tea with Lilla. Shakespeare barked at Peggy as she went inside, and she let him out into the backyard.

"Please tell me you have good news about the alarm service," Peggy said to Steve. "I've got serious issues with that trying to get the shop open again. I haven't talked to Dalton yet, but he's not going to like it that someone got in the house without us knowing either."

"There are twenty-four hundred employees of the alarm service that takes care of the house and the shop. I looked through their records, and no names jumped out at me, no one from the list of names at Stewart's Furs either. But I've got their employee information, and I'm having the FBI computer search through it for possible suspects. If something comes from that, we can set up individual interviews. Until then, we're still at the same place."

"Aren't you going to get in trouble using the FBI computers?" she asked. "One of us is already out of a job. Someone needs to have a paycheck."

He kissed her forehead and smiled. "It seems there are protocols set in place for FBI personnel under threat. My boss says this is my top priority. I'm using everything the FBI has to find this person."

"I understand that." Ranson nodded. "Can't get a good day's work out of someone fearing for their family. Smart move—even for the FBI."

"In the meantime, unlike The Potting Shed, whoever came in the house did it while the alarm wasn't set. We have an idea about when that was since you think it was when the supply truck got here yesterday morning. We can use that information once we have a few names to create profiles for. In the meantime, the head of the alarm company assured me that our personal alarm is safe."

"Well thank goodness for that," Lilla said. "At least that makes me feel better."

"What about those people from the shop who bought the same mink coats that killed that woman?" Ranson asked.

Steve shook his head. "None of them have a criminal record. They have no ties to this family or Nita Honohan. I think it may be just coincidence that they were there."

Peggy sat down. "Where does that leave us? Someone still entered the house and killed my tree as well as framed Paul for murder. How do we find that person?"

"We hope that evidence is forthcoming," Steve said. "Because I'm pursuing this with the full blessing of the FBI, I've been in contact with the CMPD. They're still working the case against Paul for Ms. Honohan's death, but the shop and our break-in here is different."

Everyone seemed to take a deep breath at the same time.

"I called Al today because I thought of someone on my suspect list that would be capable of everything that has happened," she told them. "Do you remember Ruth Sargent? It seems to me that she'd be the only one who knew me intimately enough to wreak such havoc. But Al checked. Ruth died in prison last year."

Steve frowned, remembering the case. "I agree that she's the perfect suspect—except for that—but death is hard to come back from. Did she have any family that you know of?"

"No. She never married. Never had any children. She wasn't even close with her family when she was in college."

"It still might be worth looking into." Steve took out his phone. "Excuse me."

Ranson squeezed Peggy's hand. "Steady. It's gonna get better."

She smiled and went to let Shakespeare back inside. She went through the basement and checked on her plants. She heard Sam come in upstairs and went to see him. Shakespeare followed her, sniffing at her shoes.

Maybe she was feeling down, but Sam was jubilant. He was so proud of himself that he'd managed to sell most of the plants he'd ordered.

"We should go out for supper," he exclaimed. "To celebrate."

Lilla agreed. "I love that idea."

Ranson shook his head. "I don't know if anyone else is feeling up to that, son. I know you've had a great day, but the rest of us are kind of in the swamp, if you know what I mean."

"Yeah." Sam sat at the table. "I suppose so."

"No," Peggy disagreed. "Sam's right. We should all go out for dinner, and then I'm going to The Kozy Kettle to hold my garden club meeting."

"Is that a good idea, Margaret?" her mother asked.

"I think both ideas are great," Peggy said. "We can't let this person ruin our lives."

Ranson shrugged, still uncertain.

By the time Steve came back from asking for an in-depth search to be done on Ruth Sargent, it was decided. They sat at the kitchen table, talking about everything, until Paul and Al got back. Peggy had already invited Millie and Hunter to meet them at the restaurant.

Steve and Al weren't thrilled with the idea, but it would've been hard to get through the enthusiasm that had built up. They went along with it—grudgingly—Al called Mary to join them. Paul called Mai, and Sam called his boyfriend, Tucker.

At five-thirty, they all got in their vehicles and agreed to meet at the restaurant on South Boulevard. It was in the new area, where the trolley had first been brought back. It was the only place Peggy could think of that was big enough to hold all of them.

It had been foresight that had made Steve call ahead. The restaurant didn't take reservations, but he and Peggy were good customers. They prepared a side room for them that normally was used for business meetings.

Hunter was waiting when they got there. She was surprised to see how big a group it was. "I wish I could've asked Luke, but I didn't want him to feel awkward with the rest of us talking about working around the police investigation. So I'm solo, all you married people. Just don't talk to each other."

Peggy laughed and linked her arm through Hunter's. "See? I won't even sit next to Steve."

"Why do I have to pay for Hunter's boyfriend not being here?" Steve asked.

Lilla put her arm through his. "Never mind them. You can sit next to me and tell me tons of exciting FBI tales."

Steve's expression was pained when he spared a glance at Peggy, but he smiled and held the chair for his mother-in-law. "I'm sure I can accommodate that request. I don't know many exciting stories. It seems like most of my time with the FBI has been spent on stakeouts and research."

Everyone took their places around the long table. Sam arrived with Tucker. He introduced the young man to everyone who didn't know him. Tucker nodded his head in their directions, his longish brown hair falling into his face. He sometimes helped Sam at The Potting Shed with his brilliant water features.

Al got there with Mary at the same time as Paul and Mai arrived. They did the introductions around the table as Millie arrived with Norris.

Peggy looked at her menu, trying not to feel disappointed that Steve's associate had come too. He might be annoying, she reminded herself, but he was still someone Steve worked with and trusted. He couldn't invite Millie without Norris—unless Norris hadn't been there when he called.

With so many people in the room, they did the best they could to help the three waiters who took their orders for drinks while they tried to decide what to eat. The restaurant's primary menu was Italian. One of the waiters convinced them to do a family-style meal which would be several courses that would serve everyone.

The group quickly agreed as the drinks were brought to the table and the waiters went to get everything set up.

"I guess there must be good news," Mai said cheerfully as she held Rosie.

There was silence around the table until Sam spoke up. "There was good news for me today. The police were finally convinced that none of the plants we had delivered to Peggy's house were giant hogweed. And I convinced several of our best customers to buy the bushes and plants I'd ordered for the fake Mary Hood."

Silence fell again when he was done speaking.

Finally Ranson held up his glass. "Here! Here! After a day like today, it's good to celebrate something. Right, Margaret?"

Peggy held up her glass too. "That's right. I'm drinking to Sam and his hard work. Thank you for being my partner."

Everyone talked for a few minutes as the salad course was served in three big bowls with dozens of small bottles of salad dressing.

Mai still looked unhappy. "But no good news about this crazy woman who's done so much damage to us?"

"No. Not yet." Steve said. "We're working on it."

Al agreed. "Good police work takes time, Mai. You have to be patient. I shouldn't have to tell you about it with the painstaking work you do."

She agreed with a nod and took a sip of her cold, sweet tea.

The double doors opened into the meeting room again. Three waiters came in with pitchers to refresh their drinks, and trays of warm breadsticks.

But Captain Hager and several CMPD officers followed in right behind them.

"What a nice family scene," Hager remarked with a smile. "Sorry to bust this up, but I have a warrant for the arrest of Paul Lee."

Bamboo
*Bamboo is one of the fastest-growing plants on earth.
It can grow thirty inches in a 24-hour period in some areas.
It is used for building materials and food in Asia. Bamboo
is stronger than wood, brick, or concrete, and its tensile
strength is comparable to steel.*

Chapter Twenty-one

"What?" Mai demanded in a shrill voice, waking Rosie
and making her cry.

"Let me see that." Hunter snatched the warrant from
Captain Hager.

"They found something else," Peggy whispered to her
father. "Something we missed."

"We'll find out what it is," Ranson said. "Stay calm."

It was all Peggy could do not to rush over and free
Paul as they read him his rights and put on handcuffs. One
of the young officers who'd worked with Paul put his
jacket on top of the handcuffs as a sign of respect before
they walked him through the restaurant.

One of the arresting officers was Hunter's new
boyfriend, Luke Blandiss. He glanced around the room, his
gaze ending on Hunter. He didn't ask, but the question of
why he hadn't been invited to dinner was clear in his eyes.

Peggy was just glad that John wasn't there to see this.
He'd never wanted his son to be a police officer. They'd

both done their best to dissuade Paul from following his
father on the job.

Seeing her son charged with murder was like having
someone hit her in the stomach with a sledgehammer. For a
moment, she had a hard time breathing and felt
lightheaded.

The waiters brought in three large bowls of pasta, but
no one was in the mood to eat. Dozens of boxes were
distributed to take the food home.

Steve went outside to talk with Captain Hager about
the arrest. Hunter left immediately so she could be at the
police station when Paul arrived.

Ranson offered to drive Mai and Rosie home. Mai was
sobbing and clutching the baby to her. She barely nodded
to his question, and Ranson escorted her outside.

Sam and Tucker told Peggy how sorry they were and
offered to do anything to help. After Steve had been gone a
few minutes, Millie went outside to offer support.

Norris grabbed a couple boxes of pasta and bread and
then stopped at Peggy's chair as she gathered her things
together.

"This is why you should leave these matters to the
experts," he said. "Amateurs shouldn't be involved in law
enforcement. Sorry for your loss."

Peggy glanced up at him, her temper working
overtime. "You'd better leave. Pasta sauce is hard to get out
of a white shirt."

He nodded—after moving his box of pasta out of her
reach. He understood her meaning.

"What happened?" she asked Al when Norris was
gone. Mary held her hand.

"I don't know yet. I'm out of the loop. Maybe Steve
can find out. If not, I'll call in a few favors."

"I can sit with you at the house until there's word,"

Mary offered.

She was slight and small, her head barely reaching Al's chest. She'd been a good friend for many years. She and Peggy had gone through concussions, gunshot wounds, babies, and then John's death together.

"Thank you." She hugged her friend. "I'll be okay." Peggy glanced at her watch. It was six-thirty. "I'm doing a plant workshop at seven."

"Maybe you should reconsider," Mary suggested. "You push yourself too hard, Peggy. I know it comes from being alone after John died. Things aren't like that anymore. You have Steve now. You have to relax and let go."

"I don't think this is the time for that." Peggy smiled at her. "But thanks for the good advice. I'll try to remember that after we find a way to free Paul."

Al and Mary both hugged her and left the restaurant with pasta and bread. Peggy went to pay for the bill, but Ranson had already taken care of it.

"I didn't know we were volunteering to pay when I suggested that we eat out," Lilla complained as they walked out of the restaurant.

"I'll write you a check," Peggy offered.

"That's all right. Your father and I aren't paupers."

They got in Peggy's car together. There was no sign of the police or Steve. Peggy had to assume Steve had driven his SUV to the police station. She wished she knew what was going on.

Norris was in front of the building. He appeared to be waiting for a taxi. Peggy started her car and left him there.

"That was rude," her mother observed. "He's an associate of Steve's, you know."

Peggy didn't respond. "I'll drop you at home before I go to Brevard Court."

"No. I'd like to go with you. You and your father have all these secret talks and adventures. Sometimes I'd like to be part of those. I guess this is as good a place as any to start."

Any other time.

Peggy sighed and drove toward The Kozy Kettle. Her mother talked about the Shamrock Historical Society the whole way over. Lilla was a veteran of historical societies in Charleston and had joined a group in Charlotte as soon as she'd moved there. The groups found graves where men were buried from the Revolutionary and Civil wars as well as searching for historical data for their archives.

Lilla had drafted Peggy for one memorable excursion during the drought a few years before. She hadn't gone back again.

"You should join," her mother encouraged. "The ladies all loved you. They ask about you all the time. So does that nice Mr. Underwood, though he's married now."

Peggy knew her mother had high hopes for getting her together with someone, preferably a scholarly man like Jonathon Underwood. That was before she and Steve were married, although they were dating at the time.

The street parking area outside Brevard Court had an empty spot. Peggy pulled into it, usually leaving those spaces for customers. She just didn't feel up to walking through the deserted Potting Shed again that day. She hoped the next time she went inside, it would be to begin restocking.

Emil and Sofia had always held her weekly plant workshops at The Kozy Kettle. It was a good way to bring in new customers for them and gave Peggy someplace nice to invite her group.

The Balduccis always baked extra pastries for the night and brewed special teas. Peggy was happy to share her audience. There wasn't enough room at The Potting Shed to have chairs and tables for her workshops without holding them in the back storage area—not exactly the atmosphere she was looking for.

She was grateful that she'd already planned this week's meeting. If she'd started to think much about what she was doing, she either would have had to call it off or start crying.

"Oh. This is where you hold your meetings?" Lilla asked as they locked the car doors and went through the wrought-iron gate that was the entrance to the courtyard. "It's very—quaint."

"They have wonderful pastries, Mom. You should try one."

Her mother patted her flat stomach. "I'm not one of those women who let themselves go to rack and ruin because they're older, Margaret. I would've expected that you had noticed that by now."

Peggy's talk that night was about planting rhizomes. Several of her group had asked her to do a workshop on the topic. Because she'd put some rhizome root stocks aside for this program, she still had her examples to show her usual group of about twenty-five gardeners. Some of them still came every week since she'd first begun.

After a chorus of people asking if she was okay, Peggy introduced her mother and then began her program.

"A rhizome is only a nice Greek name for a mass of roots that are growing underground. These roots send out shoots from their nodes to create other plants. Some of these we hate—such as Chinese privet and in some cases, bamboo. Others we love, like irises, lily of the valley, and cannas."

She took out her examples. "These are rhizomes from a ginger plant and an asparagus plant. Most of the time, these are good plants that we like to see grow well. And these are the two plants we're going to put into pots tonight."

Her listeners took out notebooks, pens, and cameras,

poised on the edges of their seats to observe her.

"Peggy," Cynthia Chappelle asked. "Isn't a potato grown from a rhizome too?"

"That's true." Peggy continued taking out her pots and soil. "A potato is said to grow as a tuber which is the thickened part of a rhizome or a modified stolon."

"For the most part, you'll be planting rhizomes outside," Peggy explained. "Make sure your beds have a nice sunny location. The best time to plant is probably around July or August. Be sure to dig down about two feet and allow three feet around, taking out the clay—and what I think of as junk soil—and replacing it with good quality black dirt that's loose and free of debris."

Peggy filled her pots with loose black dirt and took her rhizomes out of plastic bags.

"Make a shallow hole in the soil about twice the size of the rhizome. Take another handful of soil in the center on the bottom. Put the rhizome on top of the mount and drape the roots down the sides."

She held the pots so that her audience could see what she'd done.

"Next press down very gently on the rhizome to make sure it has contact with the soil. If there are any air pockets between the plant and the dirt, water will collect in that space and cause the rhizome to rot. Once you're sure about the placement, fill the hole with dirt. The top of the rhizome should be slightly above the surface. It's better for it to be too high than too deep."

"What about cold weather?" Sandy Duckworth asked.

"You should cover your rhizome plants like you do any others, with straw or other mulch—not with grass clippings because they become compacted and can also cause rot. If you want to use grass, be sure to use it lightly and change it often."

"How long does it take the plant to grow from the rhizome?" Sheila Donahue asked.

"About two to four weeks," Peggy replied.

Everyone fluttered around the planted rhizomes, ordered more coffee and tea, and took plenty of pictures. Emil smiled and held up his thumb meaning they'd had a good night.

"Peggy, I'm Janis Ryan from the Charlotte Observer. I was wondering if you could comment on the use of poisonous plants—specifically giant hogweed—that we've heard so much about this week."

"Of course, Janis." Peggy gritted her teeth at the question, but she answered calmly. "Giant hogweed is native to Asia. It was introduced to Britain in the nineteenth century because the flowers are huge and resemble Queen Anne's lace. It spread to the U.S. and Canada but has mostly remained in uninhabited areas. It is related to the cow parsnip, which has led to many sightings that aren't hogweed. It can disrupt native plants and animals because of its toxicity."

"But how does it kill people?" Janis continued with her phone held away from her, recording Peggy's answers.

"It contains linear derivatives of furocoumarin in every part of the plant. These chemicals form a bond with DNA causing burns and cell damage. They can cause blindness with even small amounts of sap. And of course, as you pointed out, used in ways none of us would use them, the sap can cause severe burning that can lead to shock and death."

Sarah Feinstein was closest to the table. "Wow. I hope we don't have any of those around here."

Peggy was done talking about hogweed. She didn't want to see herself quoted in the paper tomorrow when people should be thinking about who had done this, not reading her words and realizing she could have helped Paul do it.

"That's it for tonight. Next week we'll be talking about how to keep your hydrangea the color you planted it. Have a wonderful week."

Peggy could see Janis fighting through the crowd to reach her and ask more questions. She tried to get her things together so she could leave before the reporter reached her. She wasn't fast enough, but at the last minute, her mother placed herself squarely between the reporter and her daughter.

"I just have a few more questions," Janis said.

"My daughter is finished answering questions for tonight. Thank you for coming."

Janis tried to push past Lilla. She didn't budge.

"Dr. Lee," Janis said. "Only one more question about your son's arrest."

Peggy opened her mouth to speak, but her mother beat her to it.

"Are you serious, young woman?" Lilla demanded. "Do you really think my daughter wants to talk about her only child being arrested for murder? I wouldn't want a daughter of mine rudely asking questions of people in pain that she didn't know. Take what you have and be grateful for it. Don't make me call the police. We have deep ties in that community, you know."

Plum Tree

Plums have been domesticated for more than 2,000 years. They are still prized for their beauty and versatility, with many different varieties available. Plum trees can be grown from pits but are more successfully grown from cuttings of the tree.

Chapter Twenty-two

Janis Ryan sighed. She knew she'd been beaten by the small but imperious woman standing between her and her interview subject.

"Thanks anyway, Dr. Lee." The reporter walked away with a cup of coffee in her hand.

"Thanks, Mom." Peggy was surprised. "When did you become part tiger?"

"I grow fangs and claws whenever anyone in my family needs me." She picked up Peggy's handbag. "I can take this if you need to bring those plants with you."

"You could leave them here with us until you reopen The Potting Shed," Sofia said. "Think of it as a promise for the future between me and you."

"Thanks. I don't think it will be much longer."

Emil brought out a huge to-go bag out from behind the counter with him. "We baked extra today for you, Peggy. Take it home. Enjoy it."

Sofia poked her lightly in the ribs. "You're getting too

thin, just like my cousin Marty."

Emil crossed himself. "God forbid."

Peggy rolled her eyes as she knew a story was coming.

"Marty stopped eating when his lady friend dumped him. We told him no woman would be interested in a garbage man. The smell alone is too much. His lady moved on to a banker. Always smelled good and well dressed."

"Marty stopped eating. He thought the problem was that he was fat. We tried to tell him." Emil shrugged and glanced at his wife.

"A year later. Marty weighs ninety-two pounds. You can see every bone in his body. Are the girls interested in him? No. He still smells like garbage."

Before Peggy could stop her mother, Lilla asked, "What happened to him?"

Emil clapped his hands together. "He broke his leg on the garbage truck and had to go to the hospital. He gained some weight back and married a nurse who got him off the garbage truck and into her father's antique store."

"I guess that was a good choice," Lilla said.

"Thanks for everything." Peggy smiled at them. "I'll see you soon."

The two women left the shop with Sofia and Emil waving and calling out goodnight from the open doorway.

"You're lucky," Peggy said. "It could've been a lot worse. The last time I asked what happened to one of their unfortunate relatives, the woman had been dragged through the street and beheaded."

Lilla put her hand to her throat. "Really? In this day and age?"

Peggy got in on the driver's side. "Who knows? Let's go."

They drove home with Lilla asking Peggy more questions about giant hogweed. Peggy hoped she didn't go home and dream about the stuff. Steve's SUV was in the drive at the house. She hoped he had good news.

Her cell phone buzzed before she could get out of the car. It was Nightflyer with a brief text. "BIG CHANGE IN YOUR SITUATION COMING SOON. WATCH YOUR BACK. IT MAY NOT BE WHAT IT SEEMS."

"Was that your father? I'm not sure how he thought he was going to get home after he drove Mai back in her car."

Peggy closed her text account. "The car is here. Maybe he thought you'd come get him."

Lilla snorted. "He should've mentioned that before he volunteered his services."

Steve was waiting inside. He and Peggy hugged before he gave her the news.

"Forensics found some DNA evidence in Nita Honohan's bedroom. It was Paul's."

"That's ridiculous," Lilla said. "I'm going to pour myself a bourbon so your father won't think I can drive him home. Goodnight, Steve."

After she'd gone up the spiral stairs, Peggy and Steve sat in the kitchen, holding hands and staring at each other.

"What's his bail?" she asked.

"He hasn't had a bond hearing yet. He's going to have to spend the night in jail. There's nothing we can do about that."

"All the years the city has taken from him and John, you'd think they could speed up a bond hearing for him. He's not safe in the county lock-up."

"He's got a lot of friends with the CMPD. So does Al. Someone will look after him."

"I wish I could go and sit with him tonight." She sighed and put her head in her hands.

"I wish we both could. But there's nothing more we can do tonight to help him. Let's turn in. Everything looks better in the daylight."

"What about Dad? I better go get him. I think Mom is

serious about not going back out."

"I'll go. Let's call him first and make sure he hasn't made other plans."

Peggy took out her cell phone. Steve had been right about making other plans. Ranson wasn't coming back that night. He was staying with Mai and Rosie. Mai's parents were out of town, and she'd be alone.

"Thanks, Dad." Peggy smiled. "Steve says everything will be better in the morning."

Ranson chuckled. "If he's right, we need to get him a new job. He'd make a lot more money predicting who's going to win the next NASCAR race than he does working for the government."

"You're right. See you in the morning."

"All right, honey. You make sure you tell your mother that I'm spending the night with a lovely young woman. She'll be worried."

"I'm so sure. Goodnight, Dad."

Peggy made sure the alarm was set on the house. She was amazed that she hadn't heard from John's uncle, Dalton Lee. Usually if anything happened that regarded the house, he was right on top of it.

Dalton took care of the house trust. That meant that he was responsible for anything that needed to be repaired or replaced. He'd tried his best to nudge Peggy out of the house, but since John's cousin, the rightful heir, wasn't interested in the house yet, there wasn't much Dalton could do about it.

Peggy wanted to finish her life in this house. She hoped John's cousin could wait that long to decide that he was ready to settle down.

She cringed as she walked into the main hall downstairs. She'd have to walk past her dying spruce. As she got closer to the spot, she realized that the tree was gone. The huge container that had held it was empty.

She looked at Steve. "Did you do this?"

He put his arms around her. "Sam and I did it together. There was no point in you watching it die. You can get a new blue spruce and plant it here. Then you can watch it grow."

At first, she was offended that it was gone. Her heart was sick with it. But she realized Steve was right. Continuing to watch it die wouldn't make it any better.

"Thanks." Her voice was thick with tears. "I love you."

"I love you too."

"You know," he said before they started upstairs. "We don't have to stay here, in this house."

"I know." She wiped away her tears. "But I can't think about leaving, at least not right now."

"I understand."

But later that night when Peggy tossed restlessly in bed, she wondered if he did understand, or if she should even ask him to. She'd shared this house with John, and it remained in his family. Maybe she and Steve should buy a house together, and she should finally give Dalton what he wanted.

For years she'd told herself she had to stay here to make sure the house had someone in it. Houses without people were sad and fell apart. She didn't want that to happen to the wonderful old house that had been her home for more than three decades.

But she knew Dalton would hire a caretaker to live here until John's cousin was ready. Maybe he'd never be ready. He hadn't seemed excited about inheriting the estate. She wished it could pass to Paul, but that would never happen. Dalton had made that clear.

Where would she ever find a place like this? It wasn't just the size of the basement where she worked or the extensive grounds that she and John had reveled in upgrading and planting. It was the love with which the

house was built and the love she and John had poured into
it. It was the place she'd raised her son, and grown up in
herself.

It was a big part of her life.

But how did that make Steve feel? He didn't have any
input into the house. It would never really feel like his
home. How could she do that to him? He'd embraced her
crazy family and her crazier lifestyle without a single
question. Was it fair to keep him from owning a home too?

Peggy had no answers to the riddle. But tortured and
sleepless, she wandered downstairs to the library with
Shakespeare.

The old house creaked and groaned in the spring storm
that had come up. Rain bounced off the new roof that had
been replaced last year. She started a small fire in the
hearth to ward off the chill. For once, she didn't want to
spend time with her plants in the basement. All she could
think about was her son sleeping in a jail cell.

If it wouldn't have been for her obsession with
poisonous botanicals, it would've been harder for the DA to
make a case against Paul. Using a coat full of poison gel
derived from obscure plants as a murder weapon wouldn't
have been something that would occur to many people. But
everyone in Charlotte knew it was her cup of tea.

She huddled in a chair near the fire with a blanket
thrown around her and her dog at her feet. What was she
missing in trying to find the real killer? She was usually
good at this kind of thing. In this most important of cases, it
felt like her brain had turned to pudding.

She thought about all the facts again and her mind kept
coming back to the same conclusion—Ruth Sargent. This
had to be something involving her old friend. She was
missing exactly what it was—they all were. If it wasn't
Ruth, it had to be someone she'd spoken to about Peggy

and her family. Someone Ruth trusted had decided to exact revenge for her imprisonment.

Peggy got up and switched on the desk lamp before taking out a piece of paper and a pen. She doodled everything she was thinking on the paper, even considering asking if Ruth's body could be exhumed to be certain that she was dead.

But maybe the important thing was to check the prison records, find out who visited her and if she received any mail. If there had been someone who'd befriended Ruth, that person might be the one who took up the sword on her behalf.

The pen that had been on the desk stopped writing. She rummaged through the drawer, looking for another one. With thoughts of what she could do next, she came across an old cell phone.

Maybe not old, she realized, though not one of their phones that they used every day. This was a burner phone, as Al, Steve, and Paul called them. A cheap phone with pre-paid minutes.

She examined it curiously and found pictures on it with one call made to Al's number.

Last year, Paul had managed to find missing documents that had been taken from his father's police file. It had been his motive for becoming a private detective. The pictures on the phone were of the documents that had been stored here in the library but had gone missing with no explanation.

Paul had kept copies of the documents but the question had remained—who'd taken them from her house?

She didn't know what the call to Al said, but there was a return voicemail from him. "It's good you got rid of those files, Steve. There's nothing but heartache and danger in them for Peggy and Paul. Let's talk tomorrow."

Carrot
Wild carrot seeds were used medicinally and as a spice 5,000 years ago. The seeds have been found in prehistoric cave dwellings. The Greeks only used carrots in medicinal applications and not as a food.

Chapter Twenty-three

Furious at being duped by her husband and one of her best friends, Peggy almost threw the phone across the room. She wanted to cry but couldn't. Steve and Al had acted in what they believed to be her best interests. They'd lied to her and destroyed evidence that could lead to John's killer.

Betrayed and unsure what to do, she sat in the chair and held the cell phone in her lap.

The next morning, she was up and dressed before Steve got out of bed. She'd spent the time in the basement checking her plants and let Shakespeare out. There was coffee brewing, and the tea kettle was whistling. She'd even made pancakes for her father and Steve.

This wouldn't be the final word on the subject. At some point, there would have to be a reckoning. She was still angry and resented that Steve had tried to hide the truth from her. But whatever he'd done with those documents, Paul still had the originals.

She and Paul had read through them several times, but they were heavily redacted. They knew that John had been killed for his work with the FBI, probably by a sniper who'd been at the domestic abuse crime scene which was the last case that he'd worked.

But for now, she couldn't afford to dwell in the past. She had to figure out the case in front of her so that Paul was freed. She had to get her family out of danger and re-open The Potting Shed. There was more than enough work to keep her occupied.

Steve came downstairs in his pajamas, sniffing the pancake-fragrant air. "You're up early this morning. Too much on your mind to sleep?"

"Yes." She put more pancakes on a plate. "Oh look. There's Norris." She watched him drive up. "He's here early. You'd better get dressed."

"Is everything okay?" he asked, putting a hand on her neck.

"As okay as everything can be with Paul in jail," she responded stiffly.

Ranson came downstairs. "Mai's parents got home late last night. I came here once she didn't need me." He rubbed his hands together as he came into the kitchen. "Smart girl. Make pancakes while your mother is still asleep. Pile me a bunch of them."

"Coffee?" she asked as Steve and Ranson said good morning to each other, and Steve went back upstairs.

"You know it." Her father chuckled as he sat down with a plate. "We may have to live with you permanently, honey. I've eaten better here than I've eaten at home in a long time. Your mother is all bran cereal and skim milk for breakfast and salad with chicken for lunch. A man can't live on that stuff."

"Maybe a healthier man could," she reminded him of

his heart condition. "These pancakes have no egg in them. They might not seem very healthy, but they are. And the coffee is decaf."

He groaned. "Not you too."

"I think you could have some bad food once in a while, but Mom's right. You need to cut out some junk food."

Norris knocked on the kitchen door. Peggy couldn't leave him standing outside on the doorstep. "Come on in," she said in a resigned voice.

He walked past her. "Where's Steve?"

"Upstairs. Would you like some pancakes?"

"No. I had a power bar and carrot juice for breakfast." He eyed the pancakes with distaste. "I'll get him."

"He's still dressing." She poured another cup of coffee. "He may even be in the shower. I'd suggest you wait here."

He thrust back one of the chairs from the table and sat. "Fine. I'll wait."

"Have you discovered something about the murder?" Ranson asked.

Peggy wouldn't have bothered—she could wait until Steve came down.

"I have some information for Steve on the case. I'm sure he'd rather me not discuss it with you."

Ranson gripped his fork in a death lock but didn't say anything else.

Steve came down about twenty minutes later. His brown hair was still wet from the shower, but he was dressed in a button-down short-sleeve shirt and dark blue dress pants.

"Good morning, Norris. You're here early. What's up?"

He grabbed a plate of pancakes, scratched behind Shakespeare's ears, and smiled at Peggy before he sat down.

Norris glanced at Peggy and Ranson uneasily. "Maybe not now, Steve."

"Does it involve my family?" Steve asked.

"Yes, but—"

"Spill it." Steve poured maple syrup on his pancakes. "We all want to hear."

"All right." Norris took a deep breath. "Last night, one of the men who work for the alarm services company didn't come in for his shift. They found him dead at his home this morning."

Steve stopped eating and looked at his associate. "That could be the lead we're looking for. What's his name?"

Norris consulted his tablet. "William Joseph, fifty-nine. He worked for the company for the last year. Before that, his records show that he worked for a security firm in Atlanta."

"How was he killed?" Peggy asked.

Norris glanced at Steve, who nodded.

"He hanged himself. The ME has the body. We're supposed to have a report by noon."

"I don't know that name," Peggy said. "He might not be involved in this."

"Or he could be another cog in the wheel." Steve hurriedly finished his pancakes and coffee. "I'm going to check it out. I know you're going out today, but stay safe. And take someone with you."

Ranson grinned. "Road trip."

Steve kissed Peggy goodbye. "I'll call as soon as I have something."

"All right. Be careful too," she said.

Steve and Norris left right away, but Walter came in right behind them.

"Pancakes! I'm starving. Any chance for quid pro quo? I have some new information for you on the goop that killed Nita Honohan."

"I only have a few pancakes left," Peggy said.

"Allow me." Ranson got up from the table and went to the stove.

Walter took his place. "I wanted to tell you about this last night, but it was one a.m. when I discovered it, and you'd gone through that horror with Paul being arrested. Everyone at the medical examiner's office is talking about it. I'm so sorry."

"Thank you. I was up most of the night anyway. What did you find?"

"I found the sumac, poison oak, and ivy in the mixture all came from local wooded areas, specifically the areas around the Uwharrie Mountains. They contain a large amount of aluminum, as you'd expect, from the waste that was left in that area by the big processing plant in Badin."

"Good work, Walter." She took the file he was holding, thinking that Nightflyer had been right about new revelations in the murder. "What about the giant hogweed?"

"Actually from Canada. I'd expected to find that it was from Virginia since that's our closest neighbor where the plants are growing. They have a distinctive growth pattern in the colder climates not found in the plants I sampled from Virginia."

"Good work," Ranson congratulated. "But I'm not sure I understand how that will help get Paul out of jail."

"I'm sure Peggy would explain that it's all part of the big picture," Walter said. "It won't help Paul in and of itself. But it gives us a profile of the killer. He or she must live in or visit the Uwharrie Mountains and has recently been to Canada. Or purchased hogweed online, if that's possible."

"I don't think it is," Peggy said. "These are the facts that make the case against this person when we catch him."

Peggy thought again about Ruth. She'd lived, or at least used to live, near Lake Tillery, which was in the Uwharries. It seemed like another odd coincidence.

Sam came by to get more plants. Peggy and Ranson helped him load them into his truck.

"I'm so close to getting rid of all of them." Sam grinned, his perfect teeth very white against his tan skin. "Just a few more, and we won't have to haul any of these back to The Potting Shed when we reopen. Any word from the insurance dude when that is going to happen?"

"Not yet," Peggy said. "I'm going to give him a call this morning and get more insistent. It's stupid for the store opening to be held up this way. I'll see you later. Good luck today."

He waved as he got back in the truck. "Text me if you hear anything."

"You know," Ranson said. "I don't understand texting. I do it—but I don't get it. You could more easily pick up your phone and call someone. What makes it so attractive?"

"I think it's the secrecy factor. People can overhear you on the phone, but they can't see your texts."

He shrugged as they walked back inside. "So, where are we headed today?"

Peggy's phone rang. It was Mai.

"Dr. Beck is willing to let us take a sneak peek at the dead alarm service man the police found today. I thought it might be something we'd want to do in case we recognize him. What do you think?"

Redbud tree
   Eastern redbud trees, frequently misspelled as 'red bud', have bright pink/purple flowers in the spring. They are one of the few flowering trees that tolerate shade. The tree can grow to be twenty to thirty feet tall and is one of the first to bloom in the spring.

Chapter Twenty-four

"It sounds like a plan to me since we've wondered about the alarm company and how the problems with it might play into what's happened. I'll meet you there, Mai."

"Okay. At the very least, it will take my mind off the bond hearing for Paul this morning. The bail bondsman said we don't have enough equity in our house to use as collateral. I don't know where we'll get the money to get him out. I'm so worried about him, Peggy."

Because Peggy didn't own the house she lived in either, she wasn't sure, but she spoke confidently. "We'll find a way. Don't worry. We won't let him spend another night in jail. See you in a few minutes."

"Off to the ME's office?" Ranson smiled. "You're right about texting, sweetheart. You can hear what people say on the phone."

"Yep. Give me a few minutes to change clothes. Are you going to tell Mom?"

He frowned. "Nah. I'll leave her a note. If I'm lucky,

she won't get up until I get back anyway."

Peggy went upstairs to change clothes, her eyes drawn to the large, open space where the spruce had been. She jostled her mind away from that loss and focused on what she needed to do moving forward. It was also much easier to put the whole problem with Steve and Al away from her with so much going on.

She met her father back downstairs a short time later. She'd changed her casual clothes for something more appropriate for a visit to a place she hoped to work again soon. Her spring green dress was light and frothy, reminding her of the season of new life. It was the same shade as many of the young leaves shooting out around the city.

Her father had put on long pants instead of his shorts. He'd also left her mother a note on the kitchen table.

"Coward," she accused him with a smile.

"Whatever. What is it the kids say nowadays? Talk to the hand." He held his hand out in front of her face.

Peggy laughed as she grabbed her bag. "The kids used to say that, Dad. You'll have to watch some different YouTube videos if you want to know what they're saying now."

He frowned as they walked out the door. "I don't want to watch the educational videos if that's what you mean."

Peggy tried to explain on their way over to the medical examiner's office. She wasn't sure if he understood, but he could Google it. He'd see what she was talking about.

She parked the car in the lot, sorry in a way that she hadn't come by herself. It was such a beautiful morning. She wished she'd been able to ride her bicycle. It would have been a good way to clear her thoughts. But it was nice having her father with her too.

Meeting Dr. Beck at the entrance was an odd feeling.

Since Peggy had been stripped of her ID for the office, someone else had to walk her inside. The security guard at the door smiled and saluted, as he always did, but with a slightly apologetic air because he couldn't let her in.

Dorothy Beck was the same as always. She was happy to see Peggy and also welcomed her father.

"I'm sorry this happened." Dorothy hugged Peggy. "I hate that I wasn't here. I know there's nothing I could have done to make it different. I just hate that Mai was suspended too."

Dorothy was a tall, thin woman whose white lab coat always seemed to hang on her. She was in her fifties and wore large glasses over her attractive brown eyes.

"I'm sorry your conference had to be interrupted," Peggy said as they walked back to the area where the bodies were kept in cold storage. "Did you have a good time while you were there?"

"I only went because it was being held in Key West. It was beautiful there."

"Have you done the autopsy on this man yet?" Peggy asked.

"I started it. We're a little shorthanded." She looked at the clipboard in her hands over the top of her glasses. "The police said Mr. Joseph hanged himself, but there is bruising around his wrists and contusions on his face and head. If the killer wanted us to think it was suicide, they should've been more careful. I'm calling it murder."

"I see."

"And the police let you make that call?" Ranson asked.

"That's my job." Dorothy smiled at him. "Unless someone else is here to disagree with me. That's been one nice thing about you being gone, Peggy!"

They donned masks, gloves, and boots to go into the autopsy room. Dorothy asked Ranson if he was sure he wanted to go in. His reply had something to do with butchering animals on the farm when he was a child.

But when Dorothy pulled back the sheet that had been covering Mr. Joseph, Ranson blanched and walked quickly out of the room.

"I guess he wasn't as prepared as he thought," Dorothy remarked.

Peggy's eyes stayed on the dead man's face, her heart beating double time in her chest.

"Do you recognize him?" Dorothy asked.

"Yes. That's my insurance adjuster, Bobby. He said his name was Robert Dean."

"I don't see that name on the list."

Mai came into the autopsy room. "Peggy, I think your Dad is sick." She looked at the corpse. "I don't know this man. Do you?"

"Only for a few days. He's been coming to the shop representing Gromer's Insurance."

"Is that a good thing?" Mai asked. "Does this mean he was part of what happened at The Potting Shed?"

"Probably so. He might be responsible for my tree dying too since he could keep an eye on the house."

Dorothy asked about the house, and Peggy explained about her tree.

"We need to talk to Al," Mai said. "Now that we know that this man was going by another name, maybe the police will look at him instead of Paul."

Peggy frowned as she stared at the man's dead face. "Let's hope so. I'm not sure what role he played in all this, but it's possible it was all him." Peggy thought again about the woman who met with Paul and Sam but didn't mention it.

Mai took out her cell phone to call Hunter. It rang in her hand, startling her.

Peggy's cell phone rang too. Both women stepped outside the autopsy room to answer.

"Paul made bail," Steve said to Peggy. "He had a high-powered lawyer in court with him. I could see he didn't know the man, but I guess it doesn't matter. He's free for now."

Al was on the phone with Mai giving her the same information. Mai started crying and had to hang up.

Peggy told Steve about the new development. "I was thinking last night. Suppose Ruth Sargent is dead, but before she died she met someone—someone who was willing to get revenge on me for putting her in prison. What if that person was William Joseph?"

"I'll check it out," Steve said. "What was the name he used pretending to be with the insurance company?"

"Robert Dean. Let me know what you find. Mai and I are at the morgue right now, but we'll be leaving soon."

"This is it, Peggy," Steve said. "Ask Mai to find out about this lawyer who got Paul out on bail."

"I'm sure I speak for both of us when I say that I don't care who he is as long as he got Paul out of jail. Was he all right?"

"He had a few bruises on his face, but otherwise, he looked okay. I'll see you later."

Peggy and Mai hugged each other and told Dorothy the good news. Peggy had to look for her father who'd had to wait outside after his encounter with the corpse.

"How the hell do you two do that job?" Ranson demanded. "Excuse my French."

Mai was still wiping tears from her eyes. "It wasn't easy at first, but I do it for these moments when it all comes together. I help people find out what happened to their loved ones and put bad guys in jail. It's worth a little smell and blood to me."

Peggy agreed.

"The two of you have stronger stomachs than me. I take my hat off to both of you."

After a short discussion in the parking lot, Mai went to

get Rosie from the babysitter, and Peggy went home. She felt like holding her cell phone, anxiously waiting to hear from Paul.

It didn't happen that way. Paul was at the house with Steve and Al. Peggy immediately called Mai to let her know.

She hugged her son as though she'd never let him go again.

"Are you okay?" She cried as she put her hand on his chest and caressed his face. He was dirty and tousled but seemed to be unhurt.

"I'm fine, Mom. I had a little run-in with one of the men in lockup when the guards' backs were turned, but it was only a few punches and a scuffle. I get that most days on patrol."

They all heard Mai's car come screeching off Queens Road, almost hitting a large redbud tree as she entered the driveway. Paul ran out to meet her. Shakespeare barked joyously until Steve had to take him out for a walk to save everyone's frazzled nerves.

The couple walked inside together. Mai hadn't had time to get Rosie after Peggy's call. She'd come straight to the house to see Paul.

"How did you get out? They said they couldn't take our house for bail," Mai said. "How did you get a lawyer who wasn't a public defender?"

Paul smiled and handed Peggy a business card. "Because my mother has some unusual friends."

Peggy looked at the card with a black chess knight on it and realized that the bail money and the lawyer were a gift from Nightflyer.

Daylily
Daylilies are not actually of the lily family. True lilies grow on tall stems with flowers at the top. Daylily flower stems are called scapes. They are shorter and grow from a fountain of grass-like foliage at ground level.

Chapter Twenty-five

"How did Nightflyer know about what was happening?" Steve asked when he came inside with Shakespeare.

"I told him." Peggy hoped they wouldn't have this discussion in front of everyone.

"I thought you didn't talk to him anymore?" Steve pursued the subject.

"He knew what was going on and got in touch with me. I wouldn't turn down anyone's help in this case." She burned to yell at him about his hypocrisy. He dared to question her about Nightflyer knowing he'd gotten rid of her documents about John?

As if Steve saw the challenging, angry expression in her green eyes, he backed off.

"Well, at least Paul is free, and we have a new lead to pursue. Millie is already looking up information on this man."

Lilla finally got out of bed and was thrilled to see her

grandson there. "This is cause for celebration. I want to take everyone out for lunch."

After the past night's fiasco, no one wanted to go along with that suggestion. Ranson and Lilla left a little while later with her being none the wiser of her husband's morning activities—or eating habits.

Steve got a phone call after Paul and Mai went to pick up Rosie and go home.

Al asked Peggy if she and Steve were having problems with all the stress they'd been under.

She stared at him. "Really? I can't believe you're asking me if we're okay after you and Steve collaborated to get rid of the files Harry gave Paul last year. Did you think I wasn't going to find out?"

Al didn't look away from her accusatory stare. "We did what was best for you and Paul. You didn't realize it at the time, but I buried that information so that the cover-up for John's death would stay intact. You can't help him now, Peggy. You have a new life. Don't dredge up the past."

"You had no right to do that. Paul and I deserve to know the truth. All of this happened to Paul because the police and the FBI didn't want him to know."

"Peggy." Al sighed and shook his head.

"What he's telling you is the truth." Steve put away his phone as he came back into the kitchen. "How did you find out?"

"Paul and I knew the documents were gone from the box we got from Harry. We didn't know what had happened to them, until I found the phone in the desk drawer last night. You didn't do a very good job hiding the evidence of the crime."

"I didn't think I had to." Steve put his hand on her shoulder.

She shrugged it off and got to her feet.

"There isn't enough information in any file about John to go after the people who killed him," Steve told her. "The case isn't closed, but there are no answers either. If you start poking around in it, you could be hurt. Or worse. These people don't play around, Peggy. Leave it alone. Time has a way of working these things out."

"Not that I'll know if it happens since the two of you plan to keep me out of it. Maybe I should get a private detective license too."

"You're upset," Al said. "Don't do anything foolish right now when we haven't even solved this homicide Paul is charged with."

Logically, Peggy agreed with him, but emotionally, she still felt as though they had betrayed her.

Her phone rang. It was Sam. He needed the rest of the daylilies that were outside the house. Mrs. Schaefer, a longtime client, had agreed to take them off his hands if he'd plant them right away.

"I'm going to help Sam," she told both men. "Let me know if there are any updates."

She went upstairs to change out of her green dress and put on something that didn't matter if it got dirty. It would be good to get her hands in some dirt and try to forget about everything for a while.

Steve followed her with Shakespeare behind him. Peggy could hear Al's car leaving the drive.

"I wouldn't hurt you for anything," he said. "But I don't want to see anyone else hurt you either."

"You lied to me," she accused him as she removed her dress, replacing it with jeans and a T-shirt. "You destroyed information that was mine to deal with."

"I know. I'm sorry. I was trying to protect you and Paul."

She gazed at him as she sat on the bed to put on her mud boots. "Don't ever do that again. I can't trust you if you won't tell me the truth."

"Promise me that you won't go off halfcocked on some wild scheme to catch John's killer by yourself, or with Paul, and I'll make sure you get updates when I do. Can you do that?"

"I know you mean well." She got to her feet. "But I was surviving just fine without your protection, Steve. Just tell me the truth, and know that I can handle it. Can you do *that*?"

"Sure. Okay?"

"Okay. Then I promise to tell you before I go after John's killer." She hugged him.

He kissed her and held her close for a few minutes. "I love you, Peggy."

"I love you too, Steve." She glanced at her watch. "I have to run. I'll be with Sam so I should be okay, right— the two person rule?"

"Right. I'll call if I hear anything about Ruth Sargent or William Joseph."

"Great."

Peggy left with a smile. She hadn't told Steve that Paul still had copies of those documents. At that moment, she didn't have plans to either.

She put the last twenty daylilies in her backseat and trunk. She kept tarps in the car to protect the seats when she needed to. The planters were messy, but this way Sam didn't have to come back for them.

The Schaefer estate was on Sharon Road. It dwarfed Peggy's house. She'd never been inside, but the property was at least ten acres with a sprawling three-story antebellum home.

Emily Schaefer was a nice person too. The estate belonged to her family that had lived in the house since the early 1800s and had lived on that land since the 1700s. Her great-grandfather was one of the signers of the

Mecklenburg Declaration of Independence which preceded the federal document by a few weeks. He had also lost his life to a British musket ball during that war.

Needless to say, the house and yard—not to mention Mrs. Schaefer—were steeped in history. One of the rose arbors that Sam cared for had been the first rose arbor in Charlotte.

Peggy pulled into the expansive drive that circled the huge house. Sam was working in the back, the sun shining on his blond hair and tanned back. He waved when he saw her and walked to her car.

"Thanks for bringing these over," he said. "I'm working on the daylily bed anyway today. She said if I could get the new ones in, she'd take them."

Peggy smiled. "Because once the work on the daylily bed is done for the month, she can't do anything there again until next month. I know about her exacting schedule."

"Yeah." He grinned. "But she's a good customer. And I love working here. I talked her into planting some grapevines next month. I'm going to have Tucker put in a new arbor to the right of the carriage house. It will also be her first water feature. She's excited about it—and we'll make money to help get us through the deficit we'll have this month after not being open for a while."

"Did I mention what a great partner you are?"

"Yeah. I know. You're a good partner too. Anything new on the murder front?"

Peggy told him everything that had happened as she helped him make room in the lily bed for the new plants.

If she was looking for therapy, this was it. The sun was hot on their heads, but a cool breeze blew steadily through the city. Peach trees were beginning to blossom along with apple and pear trees. Emily Schaefer had allowed Sam to keep one small wisteria that they'd estimated had been growing there for at least a hundred years. There were pictures of it from the early 1900s.

Sam had carefully trimmed the plant back. Its trunk was almost a foot around. As the wisteria had grown, it had been all over the place with no tending, even reaching into the nearby oak tree.

Now, after careful pruning and a watchful eye on its growth, the wisteria was barely three-feet-tall and shaped like an umbrella with the large, heavy purple blossoms hanging down almost to the velvet green grass.

The fragrance of it filled the yard. Peggy took a deep breath and closed her eyes. This was why she'd opened the garden shop. Plants were what made a large part of her life worthwhile. She was fortunate to share that with Sam.

Emily Schaefer came out for a while to talk to them. She was dressed in a buttercup yellow, full-length, Southern belle dress, complete with matching hat and parasol.

"I'm going to the historical museum's tea party tomorrow. How do I look?" She spun her wide skirt in a circle and almost lost her balance.

Sam was quick to save her from a fall, his big hands going around her small waist.

"Oh my, sir!" Emily fluttered her lashes and purred at him. "My heart is all aflutter to have you so near."

Peggy smiled and assured Emily that she looked wonderful. She had no doubt that most of the women Sam worked for had high hopes of enticing him into an affair. Very few knew that he was gay and very happy with Tucker.

Sam put Emily back on her feet and smiled at her, a beautiful Viking statue of a man. "All right? You look wonderful. I love the dress and hat."

Emily adjusted her parasol and smiled at him with lustful eyes before going back inside.

"You shouldn't lead her on that way," Peggy said.

"Now she's probably never going to change that dress."

"That's crazy. And what was I supposed to do—let her fall on her pretty butt?"

"No. You did what you should've done. But do you have to do it so well?"

Sam laughed at her. "I can't help who I am."

"That's true enough."

Peggy got a call from Steve. They had confirmed that William Joseph had visited Ruth Sargent in prison. The two had shared romantic letters for months before her death.

"It sounds like she passed on her hatred of you," Steve said. "It's probable that when she died, he believed you were responsible for her death too. It's happened before. I think this may be our answer, but who is responsible for his death? I liked it better before your ME decided it was murder, not suicide."

Peggy took it in. Her friend had blamed her for calling the police once she'd figured out what Ruth had done. Ruth would have been out of trouble because her scheme had worked so well. The police would never have caught on, if it wasn't for Peggy taking it on herself to make it known.

"All right. I suppose that makes sense. Thanks, Steve."

"I don't know when I'll be back. I want to go through all of it with the police so we know down to the last detail what happened. Millie is out at the prison. Norris is still with the alarm company. If I hear anything else, I'll let you know."

"I know you will. I'll talk to you later."

Camellia
Camellia sinensis is called the tea plant since it is the most common form of the plant used for tea production. Camellia bushes are long-lived. The oldest living camellia was planted in 1347 and still blooms in China's Panlong Monastery.

Chapter Twenty-six

Over the next few days, everything became clear.

It seemed as though William Joseph had chosen Nita Honohan as his victim because he'd seen her at the fur store. He'd already had an idea of what he was going to do with the mink, according to notes he'd left behind from Ruth. She'd suggested he should add the poison mixture to a coat and give it to Peggy.

Obviously she hadn't meant that coat to be a fur. She had to know Peggy well enough to know she wouldn't have taken it.

He'd insinuated himself with the alarm service to be able to control the alarms at Peggy's house and the shop. The plan was so well-thought-out, but he couldn't have done it without Ruth's guidance from prison.

The insurance company knew nothing about William—they hadn't sent an adjuster or investigator to the break-in at The Potting Shed because their service was terrible.

Peggy decided that once everything was cleared up, she was shopping for a new insurance company.

She demanded that the company send someone out to meet her and speak with the police, threatening a lawsuit. The woman on the phone was flustered and said she'd have someone out right away.

It took a lot more to clear Paul's name and get him out of police custody and back on the job. There were endless interviews, letters from people who knew him well and could vouch for his character.

She was proud that he had endured it all with a smile and a grim determination to go back to his former life. He'd managed to put it behind him and was scheduled on the next duty roster a few days later.

Peggy had lunch with him and Mai in the sunshine by the magnolia tree outside the medical examiner's office.

Mai was back at work, and Peggy's good name had been restored. A family of bluebirds chirped from their nest in the tree. Life was back in balance, and spring was wonderful.

Dorothy ate lunch with them at the picnic table. They'd visited the Greek food truck and come back with delicious treats.

"It's hard to imagine being so obsessed with someone that you're ready to kill for them," Dorothy said as she plowed through her souvlaki. "I love my husband, but I wouldn't stalk people for him or kill someone. It's crazy."

"Especially since Ruth was already in prison for killing someone," Mai said. "I mean—hello! I'm not a good person. Don't fall in love with me."

Paul laughed and hugged her. "It doesn't work that way. People feel sorry for inmates sometimes. They believe that their stories about being innocent are true."

"Well, I'm just glad it's over," Mai declared. She left

some crumbs for the birds from her pita. "I like my life being normal. Which reminds me—have you given back your private detective's license?"

"You don't give it back, sweetie," Paul said. "And I'm not done with it. There is still a lot we don't know about Dad's death. I'm going to continue looking into it."

Mai and Dorothy both groaned.

Peggy understood, especially after Steve and Al had been so clear about why she shouldn't question what happened. She'd forgiven both men for their interference, but she agreed with Paul—she wouldn't be happy until she knew the truth.

But she didn't say that.

It was a beautiful day. Things were falling back into place in her world. Queens University had called and wanted her to do a symposium on potentially fatal plants that were coming into the area. She enjoyed going back from time to time and taking on her professor's mantle again.

After lunch, Peggy had an appointment with real employees of the alarm service and the insurance company. She was pushing to get The Potting Shed reopened in time for Mother's Day. That was always a big week for her.

The only question that still nagged at her was how William was able to get so much done. Granted that he'd hired the men who'd showed up and said they were from the alarm company. He'd put himself into a position where he could cover up the call from her shop when they'd broken into it.

It was even easy to imagine that he and Ruth had talked about things he could do to get revenge for her. Their letters mentioned the fur coat idea, but only in a vague way. There were no specifics. How had he managed to follow through with her concept on his own?

How had someone like William figured out a way to create a unique poison that would kill its victim from the outside? Not only a botanist could have done it, but it took more thought and some background in forensics that didn't seem to be available to William.

Ruth had dreamed up the project and found a way to communicate enough of it to get him through it. It was hard to swallow, but stranger things happened. And what about the woman Sam had met with at Mary Hood's house? So far, there were only a handful of men showing up as part of the plot. They had pretended to be the alarm service techs. There was also the question about the woman who had paid Paul to take the mink to Nita.

Where was that woman?

She shook her head to clear it as she negotiated heavy traffic on the streets to reach Brevard Court. She had to put it behind her. It was wonderful to be out in the fresh air on her bike again. She'd been driving too much recently.

Using a lock and chain to secure her bike to the iron rail that went up the back stairs at The Potting Shed, Peggy supposed these were the details Steve had spoken of figuring out. She'd be glad when he did. The details always bothered her.

She went in through shop. It was still too early to meet with either of her visitors. Instead she went across the cobblestones to visit with Emil and Sofia. They were still bustling with a large, lunch crowd and barely had time to acknowledge her.

Peggy took out her phone and answered emails, checking other messages as well.

One of her messages was from Nightflyer. He also left her a phone number that would only be good for that day.

She went out in the courtyard where it wasn't so crowded and called him back.

"You're still in danger. Something isn't right."

For once she agreed with his cryptic statement. "I know. I've been thinking the same thing myself."

"Have her exhumed."

"I don't have that authority. They aren't going to dig up Ruth because I say so. Besides, I've seen her death certificate. I've seen the hospital admissions form. Ruth is dead. It's only the details that are probably driving both of us crazy."

"Do you still trust your husband?" His throaty voice made it sound as though she shouldn't.

"Yes." She took in a deep breath. "He meant well. So did Al. I'm still angry, but I trust him."

"Then you're a fool. And have that woman's body dug up. Don't be stupid, Peggy. Your first thought was correct."

"Do you have any proof?"

"No. Find some! Your life still depends on it."

"Thank you for what you did for Paul." She veered off subject.

But Nightflyer was gone, as usual. The man never finished a conversation or said goodbye. She didn't bother telling him that Steve felt the same way about trusting him. There was certainly no love lost between the two men.

She'd known Steve for a long time and didn't believe he meant her harm by not telling her about John's death.

On the other hand, she knew next to nothing about Nightflyer. She'd be more of a fool to take his words as gospel than to believe Steve.

Still she felt edgy and uncertain. Nightflyer's accusations hadn't helped.

Were they too quick to jump on William Joseph as the mastermind behind this plot? Everyone was eager to get through it—especially since Paul had been involved.

The FBI and CMPD had looked at the information about Ruth Sargent and had agreed that William was simply a man who'd fallen for her and acted on her behalf.

What was left?

She didn't want to dredge everything up again

And yet there was a woman at the heart of this—Mary Hood—or whatever her real name was.

How could she find out?

Two insurance adjusters from Gromer's Insurance visited Peggy at The Potting Shed. They were very apologetic about taking so long getting there—and about imposters being there before them.

Peggy walked them through the front and back of the shop before handing each of them a detailed list of what had been lost and what had been damaged. It was interesting that they had the same response as William Joseph.

"I'm sorry, but we can't write you a check on the spot. We'll have to make sure the alarm is working again before you reinvest your money."

Lucky for her that a man from the alarm service company, accompanied by the real estate rental contact for Brevard Court, showed up before the insurance men were ready to leave.

"I'm so glad you're here." Peggy ushered them into the bare shop. "Insurance people, meet alarm people. I'd appreciate if the two of you would work out your differences on reopening my shop."

She sat by the front window as the two agencies worked on their problems. The alarm company agreed to have the alarm repaired and Peggy's shop put back online by the end of the day. The insurance adjusters agreed to write her a check—postdated—so that she could start re-stocking the shop in two days.

"That sounds great." She shook everyone's hand and gratefully accepted the check.

The real estate agent apologized for the mix up that had caused so much trouble.

"We need The Potting Shed up and running again. We've gotten a lot of phone calls from people wondering what happened. Good luck, Dr. Lee. If you have any other problems, please let me know.

When they were all gone, Peggy walked around the shop, envisioning what it would look like when it was full of merchandise again.

The lizard in the pond popped his head out to stare at her for a moment before jumping back in the water.

"It won't be long now," she told him. "There will be new fish soon."

She locked up the shop and went across the courtyard again to The Kozy Kettle. Business had slowed to a point that she didn't mind asking Sofia to make her a cup of tea.

"I'd be glad to make you tea, my friend." Sofia smiled. "And I have something to show you."

Peggy checked through her inventory list again, making notes of the various supply companies she'd need to order from. One of her plans for this year had been to order a few birdbaths and birdhouses. She'd read that bird watching was becoming very popular again and hoped to get her customers interested in watching birds in Charlotte.

Sofia came to the table with a large pink cup. "My mother always read tea leaves. I used loose tea so I could have a look at your leaves, Peggy. What do you say?"

What could she say? "Thank you."

"You are very welcome." Sofia nudged her with her elbow. "Maybe we'll see a new romance coming your way, eh?"

"Really, Sofia. You and Emil have to learn to accept Steve. We're married now." She held up her wedding band. "He's not going anywhere, and I'm not looking for anyone else. It really hurts his feelings when you and Emil act this way with him."

Steve had never said anything like that to her. It just annoyed him.

Sofia winked and apologized, insisting they only wanted what was best for her. She put the large pink cup in front of Peggy and urged her to drink the tea.

"But not the leaves. Those we need."

Peggy drank the tea, letting the leaves fall to the bottom of the cup. She kept hoping her friends would accept Steve. They might be crazy, but they meant a lot to her.

"Okay. Now what?" she asked Sofia.

"Let me see!" Sofia quickly pulled the cup toward her. "Oh! That's *interesting*. I should have known. That's not good. I'm not sure what that means."

Peggy looked into the cup too. "What do you see?"

"I see an adventure. You won't be alone on this adventure." Sofia looked up at her. "I see a man—close but not a lover—probably your son. I see danger. It involves water. Stay away from water."

"Any water?" Peggy asked.

"Not certain. Maybe. Probably large bodies of water. Don't take any boat trips."

"Okay. Not a problem."

"There is good in your life. More good is coming. You have to be aware of it. You don't want it to pass you by." Sofia smiled at her.

"Thank you. That was lovely. I've never had my tea leaves read before."

"It was nothing. My mother always read the tea leaves. She passed on her gift to me." Sofia took the cup and started back inside. "Don't forget—this involves your son and water. Be *very* careful!"

Wild Grape
Wild grapevines have either male or female flowers on each plant and require cross-pollination to produce grapes. Domestic vines have both male and female flowers on each plant and are self-fruiting.

Chapter Twenty-seven

With Sofia's dramatic dark eyes and ominous voice behind her, Peggy gathered her things and went back across the courtyard. It felt good knowing that she was almost at the end of this hard path she'd been going down. Soon the shop would be open again, and her life would be back to normal.

She went out the back door, locking it behind her. The real estate management company would let the alarm system techs in to repair the alarm. She'd be notified once that was complete.

Sam pulled up in The Potting Shed truck and got out with a big grin on his face. "I think we actually made more money piecing out all the plants I'd purchased for Mary Hood. I'm in a mood to celebrate. How about you?"

He lifted her off her feet and swung her around a few times. Peggy slapped at his hands.

"What in the world was that for?" she asked when she was back on the ground.

"I'm happy. Things are looking up. I think that's enough reason to be excited, don't you?"

"I suppose you're right." She adjusted her top and pants. "The insurance company and alarm service have come and gone. I think we're going to be back in business by later today."

He put out his hands toward her again. Peggy backed away.

"Oh, come on. Things are good with work now and Tucker. Things are good with you and Steve. What more do you want?"

A thin, petite woman came around the corner of old brick building, glancing around the parking lot as though she were lost. It was the woman from Stewart's Furs, ill-treated assistant.

Peggy smiled at her. "Hello. I remember you from the fur shop. Can I help you?"

Sam stepped in front of her. "I remember you too—Mary Hood—or whatever your real name is. What do you want?"

"What?" Peggy asked. "Sam? What are you saying? You know this woman?"

"Yes. She had me buy all the plants and pretended to be the woman who lived in the house. She might be Paul's client too. Call the police, Peggy."

"Let's be reasonable," Peggy insisted, staring at the other woman. "What's your name? What can we do for you?"

"Don't pretend like you don't know why I'm here, Dr. Lee. I want what I've always wanted, what I deserve. Revenge." She smiled and pulled out a pistol. "Let's go for a ride."

The woman had Sam smash their cell phones and

throw their IDs in the trashcan near the stairs. Peggy got behind the wheel of the truck on her command.

She felt like this was a good thing. She'd have a chance to talk to whoever this young woman was and find out what she was trying to prove. Who in the world was she anyway? Why would she want to hurt any of them?

Peggy could tell that Sam had similar ideas in mind. She knew him well enough to guess what he was thinking. He was almost twice the woman's size. He could have easily picked her up and kept her from hurting anyone— except for the gun.

"You get in too, big guy." She gestured with the weapon. "Peggy and I need some company."

Sam agreed, climbing into the truck after Peggy and the woman with the gun. They fit snugly together in the cab. From the mid-seat position, she could easily shoot Peggy or Sam. It was obviously strategic.

And if this was the woman who had masterminded everything that had happened to them, it was no surprise.

Even though Peggy wasn't happy that Sam was with her for this, she was also thankful that she wasn't alone. They stood a better chance against the woman with both of them there, if they had to overpower her. She was bound to make a mistake. Or perhaps one of them could talk her out of whatever she had planned.

"Who are you?" she asked the younger woman.

She definitely wasn't Ruth Sargent—yet thinking about Ruth made her see a faint resemblance to her former friend that she hadn't noticed in the fur shop. It was probably the new arrogance as she faced them.

In the fur shop, she'd seemed demur and shy. Now, Peggy realized, she was probably just hiding her face.

And it could explain how the idea of using the mink coat to kill her victim might have come about.

"I'm Diane Bartlett. I think you knew my mother, Ruth Sargent. The two of you were besties for many years, until you betrayed her." The tone and gaze were unrelenting.

"I didn't betray Ruth," Peggy argued. "She betrayed herself when she killed those two people. She lost herself somewhere. It had nothing to do with me."

"Right." Diane nodded. "Everyone is innocent when it comes to paying for their sins. I know what you did. Stop talking and drive."

"Where to?" Peggy asked. "What are you trying to prove now?"

"I'm trying to prove that everyone deserves their revenge—even my mother. She nudged the barrel of the gun into Peggy's side. "Drive!"

"Ruth never married," Peggy persisted, trying to confuse or break Diane's stubborn ideas of revenge down. "She never had children. Who are you really?"

"I'm only gonna explain this to you once, old lady." Diane held the gun to Peggy's head. "She did have a child. Me. True, she never married my father, and she gave me up for adoption. She had to forget about me because of what you put her through. But I never stopped looking for her. I finally found her after the murder trial. I visited her in prison. She and I were very close before she was killed."

Peggy thought about the names on the prison visiting list. Diane was probably on the list but no one would have suspected that the woman visiting Ruth was her daughter.

"Nice and easy now," Diane said, telling Peggy to turn out of the parking lot. "We're headed out of Charlotte, down Independence Boulevard to Albemarle Road. Nothing funny or blondie gets a new part in his hair."

She smoothed her hand over Sam's tanned arm. "And that would be a shame to waste such prime grade manhood."

"I had nothing to do with Ruth's death." Peggy persisted in keeping the conversation going as she inched out into the road. She glanced in the rearview mirror, hoping for once that a police car was following them. No such luck.

Was there anything she could do to attract attention? She frowned, thinking of all the tales she'd heard through the years from John and Paul about reasons they had stopped drivers even though they weren't speeding.

Broken taillights. Partially open trunks. Erratic driving. They all came to mind, but it was too late to break a taillight. She didn't have a trunk, and Diane would probably notice erratic driving.

Sam was eyeing the gun. Peggy knew he was probably plotting what he could do to get control of the gun without one of them getting hurt. It wasn't going to be easy with the weapon held at the ready in Diane's hands. He'd never be able to get out fast enough to avoid getting shot either.

"You had everything to do with it. She told me what you did. No one even suspected her of killing those people until you had to tell the police."

"Your mother was a killer too. I guess it runs in the family," Sam said.

"Shut up. What do you know about it? You and your brother have led such sheltered lives."

Sam raised his brows but didn't enlighten her that he didn't have a brother.

Peggy knew right away that she thought Sam was her son too. She'd been speaking about Paul.

Maybe he should. Maybe Diane would let him go if she knew they weren't related.

"He's not my son," she said flatly, swerving a time or two into the center lane and back to the edge of the crowded road in what she hoped was an erratic fashion.

"Right." Diane laughed. "He looks more like you than Paul does. Just drive. He's coming with us."

"What can I do about what happened to Ruth now?" Peggy demanded. "Where are we going? What will this prove?"

"We're going to my mother's house on Lake Tillery. You've been there a few times. You know the way. There's something I want to show you and Sam." Diane smiled at him. "I'm just sorry Paul isn't here too."

Sam shrugged.

Peggy knew he wouldn't tell Diane the truth now. It probably didn't matter anyway.

"It's a long way to Lake Tillery from Charlotte," Peggy said. "Why waste your time? If you want to kill us, you might as well do it here. Your mother would never have gone along with these theatrics. I guess you're not much like her after all, except the killing part."

Diane waved the gun at Peggy. "Because this is *my* plan, not yours. Shut up and drive. You never really knew my mother at all. Not like I knew her. Those murders she committed that you turned her in for—they weren't the first. She laughed when we talked, thinking about how stupid you were."

Peggy considered that Diane was insane. She didn't believe that Ruth had murdered other people. Her crime was one of passion. Those were very rarely duplicated. Diane saw what she'd wanted to see in her mother. Those ideas had made excuses for her actions.

It was an hour-long drive from Charlotte to Ruth's house on Lake Tillery.

Peggy kept driving in a crisscross pattern from the middle of the road to the edge. More than once, a horn blared at her, but Diane didn't notice. She seemed intent on their destination and what she had planned for them.

They passed several CMPD cars before they'd left Charlotte, but they didn't notice Peggy's driving either, or didn't seem to think it was strange anyway. She realized that once they left the city, it would be harder to get away or find a police officer who might question her driving.

Peggy tried to think of a way that she could crash the truck into a light pole or a tree and manage to get out without being too badly injured or shot. It seemed impossible since she had to account for Sam too. Even if the airbags protected them from the collision, Diane was bound to shoot one or both of them.

"I think we need gas before we get out of the city," Sam said. "There aren't many gas stations out there."

Diane peeked at the gas gauge. "Nice try, handsome, but I'm not stupid. The tank looks full to me. Want to try telling me that it doesn't work right?"

Sam didn't say anything.

Peggy counselled herself to be patient. There would be a moment that they'd get their chance—but probably not until they got to the house.

The scenery changed dramatically from Charlotte to the Uwharrie Mountain region. Houses were further between, set on large tracts of land. The tall buildings in the city gave way to acres of fields turning green with soybeans, corn, and hay. Houses were less expensive and modern. Many were farming or mill houses built fifty years before.

Traffic thinned out, but got slower as they followed large farm equipment down the roads and saw even more equipment in the fields that were being worked. Trees and sky were predominant and then the rivers that had been tapped for hydroelectric.

Small towns had been emptied and flooded years before to create manmade lakes that were governed by large dams owned by the power companies. The rivers in the area had been tamed for their use, as was common in all the rural areas of North Carolina. Power had brought progress to the rural areas.

It had been years since Peggy had visited Ruth's house on the lake. They'd spent many enjoyable afternoons sitting on her porch and watching the boats go by. Both of them had high pressure jobs that hadn't left much time for relaxation. A few glasses of wine from local vineyards, and an afternoon spent in the sun with a good friend, had helped.

Peggy had never understood what really happened to Ruth.

It was as though she'd de-railed and then set out on a murderous spree to kill her lover and his wife. She'd been a decent, hardworking woman all her life, despite what Diane believed.

Then suddenly, she'd lost it. There were no warning signs that she'd use her skills in underwater forensics to cover her grisly trail of death. Just as there were no warnings that she'd impart her knowledge to the daughter she'd never acknowledged, even to Peggy.

How hard that must have been for Ruth to listen to Peggy talking about Paul and his childish antics when she had a daughter of her own that she'd given up?

Maybe if Ruth had told her about Diane, things might have been different. Perhaps the new relationship she'd been willing to kill for had been more than just a fling to Ruth. Maybe she'd thought of it as her last chance for a family.

"Turn here." Diane waved the gun toward the narrow, gravel drive that suddenly came up on the right.

Peggy turned sharply, going carefully down the overgrown path to Ruth's house. She'd hoped the abrupt turn might knock Diane off balance, but she took it in stride. Nothing seemed to be able to unnerve her or sway her from her plan.

Ruth had wanted to keep this place rustic, as opposed

to her very modern apartment in the city. She'd opted not to cut a lot of trees and to keep the landscaping as close to natural as the way she found it.

The two-story house, situated on a hill high above the lake, was barely recognizable. Time and decay had taken its toll. Windows were out and the back porch had been ruined by a large oak falling into it. Scrub trees and other wild plants had grown up around the structure like a natural wall. It was mostly covered in wild grapevines and kudzu. Ruth had liked it natural, but even she would have kept the house clear of extra foliage.

Peggy knew there was a steep, rocky path from the front of the house to the water and the dock where Ruth had kept a pontoon boat and several smaller boats. She liked to go out on the lake and examine the wild life that lived there. She practiced scuba diving and tried out new methods of forensic testing, some of which had been named after her.

The lake itself had been declared unsafe for human consumption or swimming years ago. Like many of its counterparts, local businesses had carelessly dumped everything from aluminum tailings to hog waste into the water, thinking they had an endless supply to throw their trash into.

Years later, there was nothing left. No cleanup efforts could make the lake healthy again.

"Pull in over there by the garage," Diane instructed.

Peggy's hands were trembling as she turned the wheel. Sam discreetly nodded to her.

They were coming up on the moment when their best chance was going to be to get away. They had to make this count. There was no doubt in Peggy's mind that Diane meant to kill them both.

Peggy knew Sam had something in mind. She could feel his patient plotting. Sam wasn't like her. He didn't have a temper and always looked at the long game.

Would that do any good in this case? Would they have to kill Diane to get away? She'd never known Sam to hurt another living thing and wondered if he could do it.

She wasn't sure of herself hurting Diane either. The young woman was as much a victim of Ruth's insanity as the people her friend had killed.

Peggy's insides were trembling as much as her hands. She'd been in situations like this before that hadn't ended well. There hadn't been a chance for her and Sam to come up with a plan. Maybe if there had been, they'd be ready for this. She hoped Sam was ready because she knew she wasn't.

But when they finally arrived and Peggy switched off the truck engine, it was all going to be whatever they could do to distract and overpower Ruth's dangerous daughter. She prayed that she had the strength to remember what was important and protect Sam's life.

Diane made Sam get out of the truck first. "Easy there. You, blondie, get over on this side where I can keep an eye on you. Peggy, you get out over there and come this way. Take your time. Let's not make a mistake now."

"What difference does it make?" Peggy demanded. "You're going to kill us anyway."

"You, definitely," Diane said, pointing the gun at her. "Sam, maybe not. That all depends on you."

"Just let him go," Peggy pleaded. "He hasn't done anything wrong. I'm the one you want."

"He's your son," Diane growled. "Maybe that's enough. If you watch him die first you might get a taste of what it was like for my mother to die."

Peggy knew she had to create some kind of diversion that would give Sam a chance to get away. She hoped he would take it when the time came. If he ran through the woods, Diane would never catch him. But how could she convey that in a glance or a nod?

She knew him well enough to know that he was ready
to do something. She knew he wouldn't only try to save
himself—he wasn't made that way. He wouldn't leave
unless he thought she was safe too.

Sam jumped down from the passenger side. He held
his hands up as Diane moved the gun from Peggy to him.

There was an old metal gas can that had probably been
there since the last time someone had cut the grass. It was
rusted shut beside an equally rusted lawn mower.

As Diane focused on Sam, Peggy got out of the
driver's side and edged toward the can.

A thousand things were going through her head. A
thousand options came and went as she plotted to escape.

There was no one around for miles.

They had no cell phones to communicate—unless they
could take one from Diane.

She knew Diane would kill them both. Despite her coy
words to the contrary, that was a given. She'd already
killed at least twice. It was doubtful that she would hesitate
to do it again.

They had to take their chances.

Once Peggy wrapped her hand around the rusted,
broken, handle on the gas can, she wasted no time in acting.
Sam looked away when he saw what she was doing, trying
not to attract Diane's attention. He held his hands out
toward the other woman in a beseeching attitude as he got
closer to her.

Peggy lifted the can that was still heavy with either gas
or water and threw it at Diane as hard as she could.

Diane seemed to be as edgy as Peggy. The can hit her
on the side of the face and shoulder. She screamed,
pointing the gun away from Sam and toward Peggy again.

He took the opportunity and ran toward her.

Peggy hit the ground when she saw the gun swivel in
her direction. The can had been too heavy to aim properly

but she could tell it had hurt Diane anyway. She reached for a broken rake near the foundation of the old porch.

Sam made his move, leaping across the short space between him and Diane. His arms were extended and his long legs off the ground when Diane saw him and fired the weapon.

The repercussion startled the birds in the trees around them, echoing in the empty overgrown lot that surrounded the house.

Peggy scrambled to her feet to help Sam. Diane stepped back, the gun still in her hand.

It wasn't until then that Peggy saw blood darkening Sam's T-shirt. He hit the ground and rolled over several times before coming to rest next to the half-rotten garage.

Eyes closed. Not moving.

She ran to Sam's side and dropped to the ground next to him. He was unconscious. The bullet had struck him mid-chest. He was losing a lot of blood.

She turned her head to urge Diane to call for help, but before she could speak, her world went painfully dark when the other woman pistol-whipped her.

Peggy slumped on the ground beside Sam.

Stinging nettle
*Flogging with nettles is the process of applying
stinging nettles to the skin in order to provoke
inflammation. This is a folk remedy for rheumatism,
providing temporary relief from pain.*

Chapter Twenty-eight

Peggy felt herself being dragged across rough stone, dirt, and stinging nettle plants.

She wasn't alert enough to do anything to stop her attacker. The stones and plants were scratching her back and legs as Diane pulled her from the house toward the lake.

Wake up. Do something.

But though the warnings came fast and furiously into her brain, her body refused to cooperate. She could feel blood dripping down the side of her face but couldn't raise her hand to stop it.

She realized that Diane had tied her wrists together. She opened her eyes and groaned. Her head hurt—and what had happened to Sam?

Sam!

Peggy tried to sit up, grab something, and hit Diane with it. She had to get back, to get help for Sam. He could bleed to death.

Diane finally stopped walking. She glanced down at her captive.

Peggy kept her eyes closed and tried to marshal her forces to strike at the other woman.

Before she could do anything, Diane pushed her with her foot, rolling her into a boat.

"There you go. Have a nice boat ride, Peggy. There aren't a lot of people out on the water today. You should have lots of time to contemplate your life—and lack of it. At least until the boat sinks. I've been meaning to get it repaired, you know? I've just been so *busy* with other things."

Peggy opened her eyes. She was face up in an old rowboat. Her legs were also tied together. Her skin burned, raw from hundreds of small cuts and scrapes.

"Sam," Peggy pleaded. "Please help Sam."

"What's that?" Diane asked with a smug smile. "Don't worry about Sam. I'll take good care of him. I'll pull him into the woods for hunters to find this fall."

"Don't do this."

Diane pushed at the rowboat with her foot, and it slipped into the water. "Too late. Bye-bye, Peggy. Bon voyage. This kind of feels like when they sent off the Titanic. I'm making a prediction that you won't make it back to shore. Tell my mother I said hello."

As soon as the boat was on the water, Peggy felt her back getting wet. The rowboat was slowly sinking into the lake. She had no idea how much time she had.

She looked up into the clear blue sky as the boat lazily meandered into the lake. The currents seemed to keep it close to the edge of the water for a while. Overhanging tree limbs would keep anyone from noticing it. She'd never been to a lake where there weren't a few abandoned boats that had got free from their moorings.

The rowboat wouldn't last long on the surface of the water. It was already moving up across her legs and chest. She couldn't see the holes in the boat, but it must have been a wreck, barely able to stay afloat.

The water eased the pain at the back of her head and neck. She wouldn't live long enough to have a full recovery if she couldn't get free. She tried pulling at the plastic ties that held her hands. She brought them up to her teeth but couldn't gnaw her hands free. She kicked her feet and pulled her legs apart as far as she could.

The plastic ties were very effective—they didn't budge.

"Hello?" Peggy called out as loud as she could. Her voice refused to cooperate, coming out as a hoarse croak that no one would be able to hear.

She cleared her throat and tried again. This time she was loud and strong. "Can anyone hear me? Help!"

The water was almost engulfing her, the boat sinking around her.

"This would be a good time to start bailing, my friend," Ruth said.

Peggy knew she was hallucinating. Not that Ruth would have helped her if she'd been there. In this case, seeing her perched on the thin edge of the sinking boat was enough to make her realize it wasn't real.

"Go away," Peggy told the figment of her subconscious. "Let me die in peace."

Ruth's always animated face came close to hers. "I didn't die in peace. Why should you? I died in prison after another woman stuck a dirty fork into my carotid. I was bleeding on the cafeteria floor—not a good way to die. But you...you have fresh air, sunshine, blue sky. What more do you want?"

"I can't imagine why I'm conjuring your presence in the last moments of my life."

"Guilt, perhaps? You sold me out, Peggy. That had to

be hard on your poor, self-righteous little soul."

"You sold your soul to the devil when you killed those people." Peggy said the words as she spit out water that was slowly moving up on her face.

It wouldn't be long now.

"You've always had everything," Ruth taunted her. "Plenty of money. Parents who loved you. A good husband. A son who wanted to be near you. But you lacked passion. You have no zest for life. Where's the fire, Peggy? Where's your heart?"

Peggy was going to answer, but Ruth was gone. As apparitions of her past life could have gone, this wasn't one of the better ones.

"Your life is supposed to flash before your eyes," Peggy shouted. "You're supposed to see visions of the pearly gates and people you loved that have passed over."

She screamed for help a few more times. It would only be another few seconds before water covered her face. Peggy held her head up, straining her neck and shouted until she couldn't shout any more. There was no reply.

Her voice echoed around her on the empty lake.

Peggy struggled as the water covered her face. The boat had drifted into the middle of the lake. She poked her head up for a breath of air every few seconds until her nose couldn't get out of the water.

Looking through the dirty lake water, she stared at the sky until an image formed in front of her.

"Don't worry, Peggy. You're gonna live to fight another day," John said with his familiar smile. "It's gonna be okay. I love you."

She smiled, and reached her bound hands toward him.

To her surprise, a strong grip grabbed her hands and lifted her from the water.

"Hey." The grizzled fisherman was wearing a Bud

Light hat. He dragged her halfway over the edge of his aluminum boat. "Did someone put you in here? Or is this what they call assisted suicide?"

Peggy took a deep breath of Carolina air and sputtered. "Thank you. I need your help. A friend of mine has been shot."

Poison Oak

Severity of a poison oak skin rash depends on the degree of patient sensitivity and the amount and type of body parts exposed. Sensitive body parts such as eyes, lips, and genitals will experience a more severe reaction.

Chapter Twenty-nine

Edgar had been fishing for catfish in the lake even though the state said people shouldn't eat fish caught in those waters.

"I've been eating them all my life and I'm seventy-two years old." He shrugged as he used his knife to cut the plastic ties that held her. "I figure, how long do I wanna live anyway? The fish tastes good."

Peggy shivered, despite the warmth of the day. The aluminum fishing boat was still moored beside the slowly sinking rowboat. The old boat was under about two feet of water now. She would be dead if it wasn't for Edgar.

She thought about how accurate Sofia's tea leaf prediction had been. She wasn't a big believer in the supernatural, but it was hard to ignore what she'd said.

It was weird to think of it. She knew she should be focused on getting back to Sam. She thought she was probably in shock. Her mind wasn't working right.

Had John really been there with her? Or was he a

hallucination too?

She looked at the rowboat again, trying to get her thoughts together. Of course John and Ruth were hallucinations.

Her hands and feet were free. She was going to survive.

Sam. She had to save Sam.

"Can you call the police and take me across the lake to that house over there?" Peggy pointed.

"I'll be glad to take you wherever you need to go—?"

"Peggy Lee." She gave him her hand. "I'm sorry. Thank you for rescuing me. But I have a friend over there that's been shot and may be dying."

"Is that Peggy Lee like the singer?" He grinned. "I love her stuff."

"No. I'm a botanist. Lee is my married name."

It struck her that she hadn't gone back to her maiden name when John had died, but she also hadn't taken Steve's name when they'd married. How did he feel about her still having John's name?

It was another stupid, random thought probably brought on by shock and fear. She shook her head and focused.

"Let's head on over there." Edgar turned on his trolling motor. "I can't call the police. I don't have a cell phone with me. We could go back to my place and use the house phone first, if you like. That's the best I can do."

Peggy needed to get to Sam, but she also needed medical response and police at Ruth's old house. She chose to go to Edgar's place first and get help. There wasn't much she could do for Sam by herself.

The trolling motor was so slow. Peggy felt as though she might burst with impatience every minute it took them to get across Lake Tillery and reach Edgar's cabin.

I'm so sorry, Sam. Hang in there. Help is coming.

Peggy wiped away tears that slipped from her eyes. She prayed he was still alive. It had been a while, maybe an hour or more. She never wore a watch, relying on her cell phone which Diane had destroyed.

"Do you know what time it is?" she asked Edgar.

"Nope. Sorry, ma'am. I have a clock at the house too, though. I don't like to be reminded what time it is when I'm fishing."

"Thanks anyway."

The steady hum from the trolling motor seemed to have gone on forever by the time they reached the hazardous-looking dock at Edgar's place. The cabin, close to the edge of the water, was in about the same condition. A large German shepherd barked beside a door that was almost hanging off its hinges.

"What a quaint little place," Peggy struggled to say something nice about her rescuer's shack.

"I like it." Edgar offered her his hand to get out of the boat after he'd jumped on the dock. "My wife won't come out here at all since there's no indoor plumbing. That makes it all the better for me. I have to cut grass, paint siding and clean out gutters at our house in Albemarle. I don't want to do that stuff when I'm out here, you know?"

"I understand. My late husband was a fisherman too. When he was out on the lake, all he wanted to do was fish."

"He had the right of it, Peggy. Let me get you to the phone, and then we can take a ride in the truck around the lake and see if we can help your friend while we wait for the paramedics to get there."

"Thank you, Edgar."

"Yes, ma'am. Sorry about the loss of your husband. It's something we have to live with—knowing we might lose them at any minute."

"Yes. It is."

They ducked inside the cabin door, and Edgar pointed

to the old green rotary dial phone.

Peggy eagerly grabbed the handset and immediately looked for buttons to call 911. There weren't any.

She impatiently stuck her finger in the nine hole on the dial and watched as the circle went around until she could dial the next number.

How had anyone ever lived this way?

"County 911 operator. What's your location and emergency?"

She wasted no time telling the operator where to find Sam. She still had to answer more questions before the operator let her go. *Who was shot? Where was the shooter? Who was she?*

Finally, when she thought the woman had enough information, she hung up.

"I'm ready if you'll take me to my friend's house," she said.

Edgar had pulled out an old rifle. He carefully loaded it and then nodded.

"I'm ready. Just getting prepared in case this woman who shot your friend is still around."

"I think she's probably long gone." That truth presented its own problems. How would they ever find Diane? She could be anywhere by now.

Peggy sighed as she got in Edgar's pickup. It smelled like old fish and bacon.

She had to remember that it wasn't as important to find Diane as it was to save Sam. At least for the moment. But if they didn't locate her and put her in jail, she could be right back again killing people for whatever her motives were at that time.

The old pickup was almost as slow as the trolling motor had been. It kept backfiring every time Edgar tried to get it up above thirty miles an hour. Edgar apologized as they went slowly around the side of the lake.

"Thank you for doing this," Peggy said. "Sam would have no chance at all if we couldn't get to him."

He patted her hand. "Don't fret. We might go slow, but we'll get there. I hope the emergency people are faster than we are. Sometimes it can be like pushing a boulder uphill to get help out here."

Peggy was beginning to feel the effects of being hit in the head, dragged down a hill, and almost drowned. She dozed off until her head met the window next to her. She jerked herself upright then, and concentrated on the road.

It was twenty minutes until the old pickup turned into Ruth's overgrown driveway. It bumped up and down as Edgar pushed it into the area by the garage behind the house where she'd left Sam.

Peggy jumped out before the truck stopped. "Thank you again."

"Hey now. Hold on a minute. I don't see your friend who was shot. Where is he?"

She stared at the spot where Sam's blood was still on the ground.

"She said she was going to hide his body in the woods." Peggy glanced around. The house was completely surrounded by trees. "I guess he could be anywhere out here."

Edgar got out of the truck, rifle in hand. "Don't you worry. I'll help you find him.

Pine

Pine trees are widely distributed throughout the world. Pine nuts, which are extracted from the pine cone, are edible and often frozen to preserve their flavor. The Italian pine nut was brought to America by immigrants. It became a craze along the East Coast in the early 1930s.

Chapter Thirty

Peggy and Edgar were searching through the trees when the ambulance and two county sheriff cars arrived.

She ran to tell them what had happened. The paramedics took one look at her bruised and bloody face and arms and tried to lower her to a stretcher to take her to the hospital right away.

"That's not happening," she said. "We need to find my friend, Sam Ollson. He was shot here at least two hours ago. That's his blood on the ground."

She explained everything as the deputy sheriffs and paramedics listened carefully.

"I just got the missing person call on you, Dr. Lee," a deputy sheriff told her. "The FBI and Charlotte PD are looking for you."

"There was supposed to be a light green truck," the other deputy said. He read off the make, model, and license number. "Is that you?"

"There needs to be a search for that truck. The woman

who tried to kill me and my friend is probably driving it right now." Peggy gave them Diane's name and description. "But right now, my friend is bleeding to death out here in the woods. Can you organize a search team for him?"

The deputies called it in. Peggy borrowed a cell phone from one of the paramedics and called Steve.

"Where the hell are you?" he demanded. "I've been going out of my mind after I found your bike and smashed cell phone at The Potting Shed. What's going on, Peggy? Where's Sam? Are you okay?"

She started to cry, hated herself for it, and pinched her nose until she stopped sniffling.

"I'm fine. We were kidnapped by Ruth Sargent's daughter. She's the killer. Sam is with me. She shot him and then hid him somewhere. I can't find him, Steve. I don't know if he's alive or dead. Please come out and bring as many people with you as you can."

"Where are you? Did you call local law enforcement?"

Peggy gave the phone to one of the deputies. "Could you talk to someone from the FBI, please?"

The paramedics kept harassing her about going to the hospital. She ignored them and headed into the woods with one of the deputies. He'd tried to convince her to stay with the ambulance or go to the hospital. She flatly refused and told him that Edgar was out in the woods with her, before they got the wrong idea about him.

Peggy, Edgar, and two deputies scrupulously searched the heavily-wooded area around Ruth's house. There was no sign of Sam.

They regrouped back at the garage about an hour later.

"I didn't see any blood trail leading from this spot," one of the deputies said. "If he's out there, the woman did a good job hiding him. We need to call in the dogs. They'll find him."

"How long will that take?" Peggy asked.

"Not sure, ma'am," the deputy said. "We'll have to put in a request and then wait until the dogs and their handler get here. He's a local man. He knows these woods and he's real good at tracking."

Two more SUVs arrived on the scene. It was Steve and Al.

Steve jumped out of the driver's side of the first vehicle and ran to Peggy.

"Are you okay? You need a doctor." He hugged her as though he would never let her go again.

She winced from the cuts on her back. "I'm fine."

"I tried to get her in the ambulance," a paramedic said. "She's not having it."

"Go with him," Steve urged her. "You're not going to help anyone by keeling over out here."

"No." She wasn't arguing about it. "I'm not going anywhere until we find Sam."

He rubbed his hand around the back of his neck. "All right. I brought some guys out with me from Charlotte. Let's find him."

Paul and Al were in the second SUV with eight CMPD officers. They both stopped to try to convince her to go to the hospital.

Al grunted and walked away when she told him no.

Paul shook his head. "And people say I'm stubborn. It's only because they haven't met you, Mom."

"Thanks. I'm going back out now that reinforcements are here. I'm really scared for Sam. I hope he's still alive."

He carefully hugged her, mindful of the blood on her back. "We'll find him. Don't give up. Remember when Dad used to say that? It was his mantra. I always remember him saying it when I was a kid."

Peggy thought again about her vision of John. "Yes, he always said that."

Two more groups of civilian volunteers arrived to help with the search. Usually once the FBI arrived, they took over the scene. Steve didn't try to usurp the county's territory. The deputies coordinated the search in quadrants around the lake.

Peggy was in the woods again with Edgar. She introduced him to Paul.

"You know, there's just no way Diane dragged or carried Sam further into the woods," she told them. "He's a big guy, and she wasn't that strong."

Edgar nodded. "She probably buried him out here, closer to the house. Anyone could get that done. We're probably out too far."

Peggy's heart felt like someone was squeezing it in her chest. She had a hard time breathing, but didn't dare say anything if she wanted to stay.

They heard the sound of dogs baying in the distance.

"Sounds like another search party," Paul said. "If he's out here, they'll find him, Mom. They're trained to smell blood."

"I'm gonna head back now, Peggy," Edgar said. "Sorry for your friend. My wife is probably worried about me."

"You could use my cell phone, sir, to call her," Paul offered.

He grinned. "If I do that, she'll want me to have one out here all the time. It's better for her to worry about me than to ruin a perfectly good fishing shack."

Peggy hugged him and thanked him again. He gave her his full name and phone number in Albemarle so she could let him know when they found Sam.

"You were lucky, Mom," Paul said after Edgar was stomping back through the woods toward the house. "We could be looking for *you* too."

"I didn't have much choice in this. I did the best I

could," she told him. "How was I supposed to know that Ruth had a daughter who was even more devious and deadly than she was?"

"Yeah, I suppose."

"I guess I could've looked the other way when I found out that Ruth had killed those people. Or you didn't have to help Diane by getting your private investigator's license."

"I see your point."

They continued through the woods, carefully examining any spots that looked higher than the land around them.

"I don't think we're going to find Sam." Her voice was barely a whisper. Tears started to her eyes. She barely had the strength to wipe them away.

"Sure we will. It's probably gonna take a while, but we'll find him."

"We don't have a while," Peggy said. "*He* doesn't have a while. I hate that he got trapped in this. She thought he was my other son. I've felt like that about him for years. I never said anything because I didn't want him to think I was being too maternal or something. He's been such a big help...and he's so dear to me."

"You'll have a chance to tell him," Paul insisted. "I believe it. There are lots of us out here. We'll find him."

But the afternoon wore on until evening, and there was no sign of Sam.

The trackers had been there for hours with the dogs, but they kept following false trails and heading back to the garage. The trackers asked her for something that belonged to him. Paul drove back to Charlotte and brought one of Sam's T-shirts with him.

Tucker came with him too.

Paul cut up the T-shirt and gave the pieces to the trackers.

Peggy was too sore to hug Tucker. She smiled at him and patted his hand. They both had tears rolling down their cheeks.

"How are we ever gonna find him out here?" Tucker was overwhelmed by the hundreds of acres of rocky, forested terrain around them. "What can I do?"

"Everyone is searching for him. Maybe now that the dogs have something with his scent, that will make a difference. It'll be dark soon. I don't know if they'll search at night or wait until tomorrow."

"Can he hold out that long after he was shot?" Tucker asked.

"I don't know," she admitted. "We just have to hope."

Columbine
Columbine flowers are edible. The flower's meaning is seduction. There are more than 60 species of this plant, probably because they adapt well to almost every growing condition.

Chapter Thirty-one

They called the search off at dark. There were very few lights in the area, and it was too risky taking the chance that someone could fall in the lake or hurt themselves on the sharp stone outcroppings.

Peggy died a little inside when the sheriff announced that the search would go on in the morning, but it would probably be a recovery effort. Most people there didn't believe that Sam would survive the night.

She and Steve booked a local motel for themselves and the FBI agents who'd come out from Charlotte. Al did the same with the CMPD officers who'd stayed the night to get an early start in the morning.

Every effort was being made to find the Potting Shed pickup, but nothing had showed up as of eight p.m. when they called off the search. It was as though Diane and Sam had disappeared.

Peggy unwound enough to take a warm shower and get into the pajamas that Paul had brought back from Charlotte

for her. He'd also fed Shakespeare and taken him for a
walk.

She knew she was a mess when she got out of the
shower. Her face was bruised and swollen. So were her
neck and shoulders. Her arms, legs, and back had been cut
and burned by the stinging nettle.

The expression on Steve's face said it all.

"I know," she said. "I left the mirror steamy so I
couldn't see what a horror show I am."

"I got some food while you were in there," he told her.
"I thought you might not want to go out."

"Thanks."

"I've got some bandages and antibiotic ointment too,
unless you want to head over to the hospital."

She responded with a frown and raised brows.

"That's what I thought." He put the plastic bag with
medical supplies on the table. "You should probably eat
something first. Then let's take a look at the damage."

There were a few deep lacerations on her legs and back
where the sharp stones had torn into her flesh. Steve said
they weren't deep enough to need stitches and applied the
ointment gently, adding a bandage where it was necessary.

"You're very good at this," she said, lying lazily on the
motel bed. "I should hire you full-time."

He smiled as he helped her up. "I think we already did
that. How do you feel?"

"Tired. Disgusted. Stupid."

"Why stupid?" He sat beside her on the bed.

"Because I should've seen this coming. I should've
recognized Diane—I was carrying Ruth's image around in
my brain thinking she was responsible—her daughter
resembles her. Why didn't I see it?"

"That's being kind of hard on yourself, isn't it? How
would you have thought of Ruth having an illegitimate

daughter who wanted revenge? And as for her dragging you and Sam out here, no one could've seen that coming."

"I don't know." She got up and paced the floor, rearranging the dusty, plastic columbine plant on the table. "I feel like I led Sam into this. If he's dead—"

"We don't know that yet." He carefully put his arms around her. "Don't borrow that trouble, Peggy. It will be here soon enough tomorrow."

They turned off the lights and went to bed. Peggy fell asleep right away.

Her dreams were troubled by the actions of the day— except for one dream about John.

In her dream, they were together, drifting down a river in an elaborate houseboat.

"This is the life, huh, Peggy? Just floating, sleeping, catching a few fish. What more could anyone want?"

"You're right," she murmured. "This is perfect."

Sam went by them in a canoe that was suddenly out of control as it approached an area of rapids leading to a waterfall. He called again and again for her help. Peggy smiled and closed her eyes, ignoring him.

Then she and John were in the whitewater too. They were struggling to stay afloat. Ruth and Diane had turned into mermaids with sharp teeth. The women grabbed at them with clawed hands, trying to pull them under.

Peggy sat up, gasping for breath. She was grateful for the daylight that was pouring in through the motel windows. She realized where she was and went to get dressed.

All the volunteers looking for Sam met in the motel restaurant. Hunter and her parents were there too. The police had no doubt called them as Sam's next of kin.

Please let him be alive.

The county sheriff had begun speaking as Peggy made her way around the group to where Hunter and her parents stood.

What could she say to them? It was her fault that their wonderful son was in danger, or worse. Still she felt obligated to say something. They were Sam's parents no matter what. She didn't want to just ignore them.

"I'm so sorry, Mr. and Mrs. Ollson." Peggy kept her voice to a whisper as the sheriff outlined the areas on a map where they would be searching for Sam. "I'm sure we'll find him today."

Mrs. Ollson—very tall and blond like her children—turned on her with murder in her blue eyes. "Why are you here? You destroyed Sam's life. That wasn't enough. You had to expose him to enemies of yours who wanted to kill him. Stay away from my family."

Hunter pulled Peggy away from her mother. "You can't talk to her right now. She's crazier than usual. Has there been any word at all about Sam?"

"Not as far as I know."

The sheriff finally ended his report on a grim note. "I'm afraid we doubt that Mr. Ollson is alive this morning due to the extent of his injuries. But let's bring him home for his family. Be sure to check every inch as carefully as possible."

A few members of the local press had joined them. "What about Mr. Ollson's killer?" A short, thin woman with a large microphone pushed forward to reach the sheriff. "Have you located her?"

The sheriff grimaced. "We have no comment on that right now. We'll keep everyone informed as word comes in."

Steve's phone rang. Peggy saw him step out of the group that was conferring with the sheriff's department. He had an odd look on his face. She was already moving toward him, around the crowd packed into the restaurant. Her heart was beating wildly in her chest.

Steve beckoned to her across the room. Was it finally good news?

She reached him. "What is it? Is it something about Sam?"

Her words had been louder than she'd anticipated. Everyone stopped talking and stared in their direction.

"It's Selena," Steve told Peggy, his brown eyes riveted on her face. "You should talk to her."

Peggy started to ask why she hadn't called her cell phone and then realized it was because her cell phone was dead. Her hands shook as she took the phone from Steve, wondering why he'd interrupt the meeting for a phone call. It had to be important.

"What's wrong, Selena?" All eyes were on her now.

"I'm at the shop. You know how you said I should check on the alarm system this morning."

Peggy had completely forgotten with everything else that had happened. "Is it working?"

"Yes. I almost couldn't shut it off."

"But I guess you did," Peggy said. "Thank for going in."

"I got this weird message on my laptop. It actually came from the phone in The Potting Shed."

"Selena, I'm sorry. I guess no one told you about Sam."

"Sam? Was he in an accident? Is that why the wrecker service is calling about the truck? What happened, Peggy? Why am I always the last to know everything?"

Gingko

Ginkgo comes from the Japanese word ginkyo, which means "silver apricot," a reference to the fruit, frequently eaten in Japan. This beautiful, hardy tree with its attractive, fan-shaped yellow leaves, was once thought to be extinct but was rediscovered in China during the mid-1700s. It is now planted as an ornamental tree around the world, with no danger of extinction.

Chapter Thirty-two

"Wrecker service?" Peggy grabbed Steve's hand. "Where is it? What did they say?"

"I'll text you the number. Why aren't you answering your phone?"

"Text it to Steve. I'll fill you in, I promise." Peggy handed the phone back to Steve.

"Would you care to share with the group, Dr. Lee?" the sheriff asked.

"A wrecker service has my truck—the one that was missing from the scene at Lake Tillery. It's possible they know something about Sam and Diane."

Everyone started toward the door at once.

"Hold on now. Let's give the wrecker service a call before we all run out there," the sheriff suggested. "Agent Newsome? Could you relay that information?"

"Gladly." Steve pushed the phone number that Selena had just texted him. He put the phone on speaker, and the room became deadly quiet.

"A and R Wrecker Service," a man's voice said. "This is Arnie."

"This is Agent Steve Newsome with the FBI. I'm looking for information about a green Ford pickup you picked up. It has the words 'Potting Shed' on the side."

"Oh yeah. It's a mess. Took a header into a tree. Was it involved in a drug deal or something? Because I haven't done anything to it except go through the information in the glove box to find someone to call about it."

"What about the driver?" Steve asked.

"The driver was in pretty rough condition, according to the highway patrol. They'd already taken him and his passenger to the hospital by the time I got there. I don't know anything about that. Sorry."

"Where are you located?" Steve asked.

"I'm in Norwood, right downtown, if you want to get the truck. I'll be here all day."

"Thanks, Arnie."

A cheer went up from the searchers. Sam's parents broke down in tears.

But Peggy knew it wasn't over yet. Were they sure it was Sam? How could he have been driving in the condition he was in? What if it wasn't Sam and they took the valuable time away from the search?

The sheriff was already on the phone with the highway patrol.

"Didn't anyone check with the hospitals around here?" Al asked.

"That was one of the first things they did," Steve said. "We checked too. It has to be that the highway patrol found the truck later."

The sheriff held up his hand for quiet.

"I've been in contact with the highway patrol. They did find the wrecked vehicle off in the woods late yesterday. A man and woman were taken, alive, to the hospital in Albemarle. We're getting an update on their status now."

One of the sheriff's deputies shook his head, his cell phone to his ear. "They have three accident victims from yesterday with no ID. Not sure if they're who we're looking for or not. Someone is gonna have to go down there."

The sheriff dismissed all the search groups from the county since none of them knew Sam. He thanked them for their time and effort.

It was happening so fast—Peggy was terrified and wanted to call them all back.

What if it isn't Sam?

Al and Paul with the officers from CMPD were still there with the FBI agents and about a dozen sheriff's deputies.

"Agent Newsome, maybe you can come with us. One of the relatives can ride along with us since you can make a positive ID," the sheriff said. "Which one of you wants to go?"

"Dr. Lee is really the best one to go since she can also ID the woman who attacked her and shot Sam Ollson," Al said. "I'll take my people back to Charlotte and save the city some money."

Paul wasn't happy with that plan. He didn't want to leave Peggy until it was over.

Steve traded spots with Paul in the back of the sheriff's car. "I'll take my people back to Charlotte too and come back for my wife."

Peggy was good with that plan and ready to go. Sam's parents and Hunter had already left for the hospital.

All the sheriff's deputies left the motel. The sheriff waited for Peggy and Paul.

Steve kissed Peggy and made her promise to call as soon as she could.

She hugged him. "Thanks for letting Paul go."

"He needs to be there to see the end of this." He squeezed her hand. "Be careful."

She hopped into the back of the sheriff's car with her son. "As soon as I know something, I'll call."

One advantage to riding with the sheriff was that he put on his lights and siren and traveled down the highway toward the hospital at eighty miles an hour. They passed Sam's parents in only a few minutes—even with Hunter driving.

"Don't be disappointed if this doesn't work out the way you hope," Paul whispered. "I don't know what we'll find when we get there."

"It has to be Sam. No one mentioned anyone being dead from the wreck," she said. "I have high hopes that I refuse to let go of for now."

He smiled. "Me too."

They were at the hospital in downtown Albemarle about twenty minutes later. Gingko trees, bright with yellow leaves, lined the sidewalk and the front of the building.

Several of the deputies who'd been at the motel had come to join them.

Peggy was surprised to see them until Paul reminded her that this would be a big collar for the local sheriff's department.

"I'm sure they're excited to be here."

"But what about Nita Honohan's death? She was in Mecklenburg County with William Joseph."

He shrugged. "I'm sure they'll work it out so the credit is spread around—if Ruth's daughter is still alive."

The sheriff hurried into the hospital with Peggy and Paul beside him. Four deputies followed them. At the patient services desk, the sheriff paved the way for them to visit each of the patients without ID who'd been brought in during the last twenty-four hours.

Peggy was so nervous. She almost forgot how sore she was. Her legs protested as she stood waiting for the hospital administrator to come down and okay their request.

Paul held her hand, but his face was grim, no doubt thinking of facing the woman who'd tried to ruin his life and wondering what kind of condition Sam was in.

The hospital administrator shook hands all around and instructed his staff to give them the access they needed. A nurse picked up four charts and escorted them to the first room.

There seemed to be many empty rooms in the small town hospital. They passed several of them before they came to the first occupied space.

Hunter and her parents had arrived during that time and were arguing loudly with the hospital staff about being allowed to see Sam. Since there was no one with his name on the patient list, the nurses were asking them to leave.

The patient in the first room was an elderly man who'd been injured in a crash. They all backed out of his room, trying not to disturb him.

Peggy took pity on Sam's family and went back to the nurse's station to get them.

"They're with us," she told them.

"We are *not* with you," Sam's mother disagreed.

The nurse at the computer arched her brow. "If you aren't with the sheriff's group, I can't let you go looking through the all the rooms for your son. I'm sorry."

Sam's father, taller than Sam and Hunter, but without their muscular build, appealed to his wife. "If we want to see our son, we'd best go with Peggy."

Mrs. Ollson ground her teeth in frustration but finally admitted that they were all together. "But as soon as we find Sam," she assured Peggy, "we're getting him out of here and away from you."

Peggy didn't comment on her remark. Hunter whispered a *thank you* as the four of them joined the sheriff and Paul waiting for them to go to the next room.

The nurse led the way again, consulting her patient chart, and stopped in the next room up. "This is our Jane Doe who was injured in the accident yesterday."

She pushed open the door and Peggy stepped back, her hand at her throat.

"That's her. That's Diane Sargent. She's the woman who tried to kill me and shot Sam."

Diane was unconscious, with severe bruising to her face. Her nose was swollen, possibly broken. Peggy wondered if the airbag had done that damage. But she was also glad that Diane wasn't awake. She wasn't sure if she could face her yet.

The sheriff instructed two of his deputies to stay with Diane.

"Does that mean Sam is actually here somewhere?" his mother demanded. "What kind of hospital is this anyway? How can you not know who your patients are?"

The young nurse's jaw tightened, but she didn't argue. She continued down the long hall to the next room.

Paul had stayed behind at Diane's room for an extra moment, staring at her. He re-joined them with a shake of his head as Peggy silently queried him with a lift of her cinnamon-colored brow. "I just wanted a good look at her."

Peggy nodded, understanding, as the nurse opened the next occupied room.

"John Doe," she said. "Also the victim of an accident yesterday."

None of them needed the overhead light switched on to recognize Sam's tousled blond head resting against the white pillow.

"Oh my God!" His mother screamed and ran to his

side.

Everyone surged into the room, the deputies taking out cell phones and notebooks to question him.

"You'll have to wait until you have approval to talk to him, unless you're family," the nurse said.

"We're the only family he has here," his mother said disdainfully.

All the fuss awakened Sam. He blinked sleepily at the people in his room. His blue eyes landed on Peggy's bruised face, and he called her name. "You're alive."

Peggy ignored his mother and went around her to talk to Sam. "So are you. How are you? What happened? How did you end up in the truck with Diane?"

He reached out and pulled her close. "I'm okay. A little banged up, like you. I was so worried about you. When Diane came back up the hill without you, I managed to knock her down and take the gun. The only thing I could think of was to get the police since we had no cell phones. She wouldn't tell me where you were."

"Save your strength," Sam's mother advised. "You've been through a lot."

She glared at Peggy.

"She tied me up and put me in a sinking boat." Peggy ignored his mother as she wiped tears from her eyes. "A fisherman rescued me. I came back for you, but you were gone."

"I made her get in the truck, and we started toward Norwood. I don't know what happened after that." Sam shook his head. "I guess I blacked out. Since I was driving, the truck went into a tree. Did Diane get away?"

"No. She's in another room." Peggy kissed the side of his face. "I'm so glad you're all right. I have to call everyone to let them know. I think your mother needs your attention now anyway. I'll be back."

"I'll be here."

Peggy started to go but turned again. "I love you, Sam.

I haven't said it before. But it's true. You're like a son to
me."

He grinned. "Of course I am. I love you too, Peggy."

Red Spruce
The red spruce was logged almost to the point of
extinction during the late 1800s and early 1900s. Red
spruce once dominated the highest elevations of West
Virginia, covering more than 500,000 acres. Now only
about 30,000 acres of high elevation red spruce remain.
Efforts are underway to re-populate the red spruce in West
Virginia and other places.

Epilogue

Ten days later, Peggy was at The Potting Shed with
Selena putting in new supplies. Emil and Sofia were
helping, when they weren't busy at The Kozy Kettle.

The shop was beginning to look like its old self again.
Everything was so new and fresh. The little lizard watched
from the pond lip as they moved boxes and crates of
supplies around the shop and emptied them.

"When's the grand reopening day?" Selena asked for
the tenth time.

"Thursday," Peggy said. "I hope you don't have any
tests that day."

"Even if I did, I'd tell them I was sick and retake it.
Without Sam here, we need all the help we can get. He's
annoying, but I miss those broad shoulders and strong
arms."

"Is that even possible?" Sam's voice filtered from the
back of the shop as he came in with Tucker. "Is Selena
actually admitting that she can't handle it without me?"

Selena dropped the box she was holding—thankfully it

was only filled with birdseed for the new feeders. "Look! It's him. He's back."

She ran to jump on him, but Tucker held her back. "Maybe not full body contact ready as yet."

Selena stopped and stared at Sam. "You look good, Viking. Can I at least get a small hug?"

Sam put his arm around her. "Just no punches to the chest yet. I'm still healing."

The four of them walked around the shop, remarking on all the new supplies that had been put in place.

"I'm going to be kind of useless for a couple of weeks," Sam said. "But Tucker is going to fill in for me, if that's okay?"

Peggy smiled. "That's wonderful. Thank you, Tucker."

The smaller man with the long, brown hair was still a little uneasy with Sam's effusive friends. "I'll be glad to do whatever I can."

She hugged him, which gave Selena a reason to do the same. Tucker's face was red by the time they'd both released him.

"Come over for dinner tonight, both of you," Peggy said. "My dad is cooking, so the food will be good. We're celebrating everyone being alive and back to normal."

"Does that mean someone else died, and you're working at the morgue again?" Sam asked.

"No. Not yet anyway." She laughed. "But I'm cleared to work again. Mai is already back at work, and so is Paul. Good news all around."

"What about the woman who did this?" Tucker asked. "What's going to happen to her?"

"She's coming here to face charges in this county, and then she'll be sent to a state facility until her trial in Montgomery County," Peggy said. "She's got enough counts against her that she'll never be out of prison."

"Yeah," Selena said. "But can we stop her from having a fan club like her mother did? Otherwise we might have to go through all this again in ten or twenty years."

Sofia and Emil came in to help again for a while. Sofia made sure everyone knew about how accurate her prophecy had been for Peggy and Sam. Thrilled with her success, which had been documented on local TV news, Emil was talking about creating a private corner in the shop for his wife to read tea leaves for their customers.

Sam sat in Peggy's new rocking chair by the pond for the remainder of the day. The rest of the group got most of the supplies put away and then headed to Peggy's house for dinner.

It was a loud and hungry crowd by the time Peggy got back from the shop. Walter was there, helping her father cook. Her mother was drinking wine at the kitchen table with Millie and Hunter.

Sam's parents had gone back to their home in King's Mountain just outside Charlotte once their son was on his feet again. Peggy didn't feel bad about it. They wouldn't have come to the celebration anyway.

Paul and Mai got there a few minutes after Peggy with Al and Mary coming in right on their heels.

Shakespeare barked at everyone in a friendly way, excited by the crowd. Peggy walked through the dining room but couldn't find Steve. She went out into the main hall and found him beside a large, black tarp protruding from the spot her blue spruce had once occupied.

She heard the group from the kitchen follow her into the hall, but her eyes were riveted on Steve's smiling face. When everyone had settled around the bottom of the stairs, Steve asked for quiet as Walter, Sam, and Paul joined him near the large hole in the floor.

"This can never take the place of what was lost," Steve said. "But sometimes we can find things we love just as much waiting for us."

Peggy was already crying when Paul and Walter pulled the tarp from the tree hidden beneath it. It was a six-foot red spruce, long lush boughs reaching toward the skylight.

"I chose the red spruce because it's endangered, and they all need a good home," Walter explained. "I hope you like it, Peggy."

There were no words to say how much she liked it as she hugged each man in turn. She brushed her hand lovingly against the branches and smiled up at the top.

A voice called out from the kitchen as she struggled to speak over the lump in her throat.

"Peggy?" A tall man in a leather jacket and black slouch hat walked from the kitchen to the main hall. "Looks like I'm just in time for a party."

She swallowed hard. It was John's cousin, Richard, the heir to the house and property.

"Welcome back," Peggy said. "It's good to see you. How long will you be staying? I can get a room ready for you."

Richard spread his arms wide. "This is it. I'm home."

Peggy Lee's Garden Journal

Spring!

Is there anything more exciting than the world coming back to life after a long, cold winter? Every heart yearns for the sight of a golden daffodil and a red tulip. Spring is the time when we all come back to life. Just as the trees know when it is time to stretch out their limbs and burst forth with new green leaves, we want to shake off the winter doldrums and do the same.

For gardeners, it is the best time of the year. We till the soil and bring new growth into the warm air, look around ourselves and see the wonder of the seasons.

There's nothing like it!

Peggy

Celery Soup

Something great to do with leftover celery!

Ingredients:

3 tablespoons butter

1 pound of finely chopped celery

2 large, finely chopped onions

3 finely chopped garlic cloves

3 tablespoons flour

6 cups vegetable broth

1 cup heavy cream

Salt If you like) and Pepper to taste

Preparation:

In a large sauce pan, melt butter and then add celery, onions, and garlic

Cook over medium low heat until all ingredients are soft

Add flour and cook 1-2 minutes over low heat until it thickens

Add broth and bring to a boil, reduce heat, and simmer 30 minutes

Add cream, salt and pepper

Simmer 5 minutes

Feeds six – Enjoy!

Gardening

Create a bee-friendly garden!

Bees are endangered, as I'm sure you know. Butterflies and other insects that are helpful to gardeners are also disappearing. There are things you can do as a gardener to help prevent this.

Make sure that you have plenty of bee-friendly plants. Wait to deadhead as long as possible. Bees come out of their winter hibernation hungry. Plant narcissus, crocus, pussy willow, and herbs to feed the hungry new bees. Rosemary is good too! Look for as many bee-helpful plants as you can to have in your garden.

Purchase plants, bulbs and seeds that are free of neonicotinoid and systemic insecticides. These are known killers of bees and butterflies. Ask your garden supply center to have these on hand.

And keep a supply of water in birdbaths and other spaces in the garden. Butterflies and bees get thirsty too!

About the Authors

Joyce and Jim Lavene write bestselling mystery together. They have written and published more than 70 novels for Harlequin, Berkley and Gallery Books along with hundreds of non-fiction articles for national and regional publications.

Pseudonyms include J.J. Cook, Ellie Grant, Joye Ames and Elyssa Henry

They live in rural North Carolina with their family, their rescue animals, Quincy - cat, Stan Lee - cat and Rudi - dog. They enjoy photography, watercolor, gardening and long drives

Visit them at www.joyceandjimlavene.com
www.Facebook.com/JoyceandJimLavene
Twitter: https://twitter.com/AuthorJLavene
Amazon Author Central Page:
http://amazon.com/author/jlavene

25298161R00133

Made in the USA
Middletown, DE
25 October 2015